The older woman made a little sniffing sound. "Now, Peggy, you can't hide the truth from him forever, you know."

"No one is ever going to hide the truth from him," Peggy retorted, holding her voice down with an effort. "Why should they?"

"Illegitimacy is something people just never quite learn to accept and live with."

Peggy formed the word with her lips but did not say it aloud. She looked past the living room entrance where Bill and the child were busy with the electric train. She suddenly wished that Bill would come to her, hold her, right that minute. She felt an urgent need for him.

But then, almost instantly, she speculated on what effect a revelation to Bill would have. He might react with disillusionment and disgust, might even pack up and leave. And she could not bear the thought of that. Bill, now, was the one man, the only man who mattered to her.

The Aston Hall Romance Series:

Arlene Morgan

STARFIRE

PINNACLE BOOKS   LOS ANGELES

STARFIRE

A Pinnacle Books edition, published by special arrangement with Aston Hall Publications, Inc.

First printing, October 1980

ISBN: 0-523-41118-9

Printed in the United States of America

PINNACLE BOOKS, INC.
2029 Century Park East
Los Angeles, California 90067

CHAPTER ONE

SHE THOUGHT of it in a thoroughly impersonal manner as though it did not matter, as though it were one of those contingencies that are forever cropping up in life that have two alternatives—you can ignore them or you can become involved.

The trouble of course, was that those things *did* crop up. Otherwise, on the whole, life would be a lot less difficult to cope with. Every few days there was some kind of crisis; her car wouldn't start, it rained when it shouldn't, she saw starving faces in the newspapers, or, like now, they telephoned from the hospital over in Buckner to gently inform her that John Bellanger had just died.

She walked the autumn streets aware of russet-red leaves underfoot, partially aware of the chill and the hastening, low gray sky overhead, and not at all aware of the staid old homes she passed or the lights in the windows or the fact that she should have been at home starting dinner because very shortly now her brother would come home from the store as hungry as that old wolf who lived his lonely existence up along the westerly mountainsides beyond town, beyond the farms lying west of town, when she had been a tomboy. The old wolf had been gone about ten years now, and even the little legend about him had begun to die out.

She wondered if that was how it was going to be with John Bellanger and decided that it wouldn't be. The old wolf had simply been up there, seen occasionally as a fleeting gray silhouette through the trees. Except for the fact that he *had* been up there, that people had talked a little about him, the wolf really had no connection with the life of the town. John Bellanger hadn't been different; like the wolf, John Bellanger had been a person, an individual who had walked all the streets of Brunswick. He had been an authority on just about everything, including that old wolf. His little brown house with the white-trimmed windows was over there at the north end of Elm Street, and right this minute she could imagine him as she'd last seen him, as plain as day, talking to her brother out front of the store on Monday morning.

Today was Friday and John Bellanger was gone.

A storm was coming. A stinging particle of moisture struck her cheek. She stopped and studied the darkening, swelling heavens. There was some kind of enormous tumult going on up there, and if she could have been midway between heaven and earth, no doubt she would have been able to hear the rumbling, grinding sounds, but down where she stood there was no sound at all, until a woman called a child in to supper somewhere close by, her voice rising in the pre-storm hush with a kind of plaintive, fluting sweetness. Even an aggravated mother had the soft sound of love in her voice.

She turned back, and a little fretful wind came to harry her part of the way. As a child she had run out into the cascading leaves of autumn, had raced the wind with wine-red cheeks, had looked out of starbright violet eyes, full of confidence and trust because at ten or eleven years of age she'd known exactly how elemental and basically predictable life was.

Not until she was fourteen years old, the year her mother had died, had that strong confidence been shaken. Since then, there had been other shockwaves, some minor, some not so minor, until now, at twenty, she thought she understood life a little better. It wasn't a big slice of lemon meringue pie at all.

What really bothered her when something like the death of John Bellanger came up was the lack of *knowing,* the degree of uncertainty people had to live with from day to day.

A faint mist of cold rain, borne erratically inward from all sides by a scurrying little sharp wind, made her look ahead where lights burned cheerily; her brother was home. She picked up the gait a little and turned up the walk, reached the porch, and went inside.

Earl looked up from his chair in the parlor with that quick, warm little quizzical smile and put down the *Buckner Enterprise,* the only really regional newspaper around—and it was published thirty miles away at the nearest large town to Brunswick. In fact, folks called Buckner a city, and maybe that was right because Buckner's population was about four times the population of Brunswick.

Earl was tall and rawboned and wide-shouldered, the way their father had been. He had the same coarse mane of unruly curly hair, dark reddish in color. He had the kind of personality that drew people to him. He was almost always outgoing and good-natured. He liked most people and therefore most people liked Earl Wheaton. He had expanded the general store their father had left their mother, which she had operated quite successfully for seven years after her husband's death and then left to her children, Earl and Margaret Wheaton.

Earl pushed long legs out and stretched; then he said, "You picked an awful evening to go for a walk."

Margaret didn't ask how he knew she'd been out walking. She shed her coat and gloves, hung up her scarf, and with her back to him she said, "Dinner'll be ready in a little while," and would have started for the kitchen but Earl spoke again.

"Were you listening to the twelve o'clock news this morning?"

She turned, nodding.

"Then you heard about old John?"

"He died," she said, and went along toward the rear of the big old house to the kitchen.

Earl walked in about fifteen minutes later. He had washed and run a comb through his rusty hair. He watched her at the stove for a while, then went over to a cupboard and without speaking mixed two highballs on the drainboard. He tapped her shoulder, handed her one of the glasses, and went over to the window to look out at the menacing night.

She thought she knew what he was thinking. Earl was not a very complicated human being. Since they'd been children, but most particularly since their mother had died, she had taken refuge from those contingencies that came to stir the murky sediment of life by going off alone somewhere, as she'd done this afternoon and evening.

She tasted the highball—it had muscle but then her brother rarely mixed them otherwise— thinking that she did not have to justify what she did to him. She did not have to justify herself to anyone.

He turned, drained half his glass, and with his gaze resting softly on her, he said, "John told me a pretty cute joke last Monday."

She knew the kind of jokes men told one another; it did not detract from her personal feelings toward them. Old men were different from young men only in that they were raffish and sly-chuckling instead of being bold and hungry-eyed. She was long-legged, full-breasted, had hair the color of polished bronze and large, very dark blue eyes, and without feeling much about it one way or another, she knew she was better-looking than most women. She knew perfectly well how men looked at her. What had been easy friendship part way into her teens had subtly changed after that, and the boys she had grown up with, had attended school with, had gone bob-sledding and ice-skating with at Miller's pond in wintertime, had gone swimming with in summertime at Monument Lake, gradually had begun to move more slowly around her; they had started reacting differently to her presence.

Earl drained the glass and set it upon the sink. He leaned there as she went to set the kitchen table. After considering her for a while, he said, "How would you like to do me a favor?" and before she could reply, he explained what it was. "I've got a rail shipment to be picked up over at Buckner tomorrow or they'll start charging us warehousing. How about driving the pickup over there and getting it? I'd go but I'm halfway through the inventory and I'd like to finish it tomorrow."

She was willing. She kept the store's books, did them once a month right there on that same kitchen table, and once in a while, when Morris Jackson the store clerk took a day off or got sick or something, she helped in the store.

She also remembered that other time she'd headed for Buckner in the pickup truck to take delivery at the depot, so she said, "I'll go down with you in the morning. When was the last time anyone looked at the gas gauge in the truck?"

Earl laughed. His laugh, like his smile, was pleasant. "You won't run out midway this time," he assured her. "I filled it up after closing this evening."

She put their meal upon the table, and he walked over to sit down. His eyes were brighter now. When they met her gaze, she smiled at him. He could have sent Morris over to Buckner. Earl wouldn't have been a very successful diplomat, but at least it was sweet of him to try this. He wanted her to get outside of herself, to do something or go somewhere and to stop thinking about John Bellanger.

She would, in time, of course; she'd even stopped reliving her mother's passing after a while. A longer while than it would take this time.

Earl liked her meatloaf above everything else she cooked, above roast beef or steak. It was a wonder that he didn't get fat because when he sat down to the evening meal he ate like each meal would be his last one.

Sometimes she teased him about this, sometimes she cautioned him about gaining weight, but usually, as she did tonight, she simply marveled at his capacity.

He caught her watching, winked, and then went right back to gorging himself. She gave her head a mildly reproving little wag and picked at her own meal until he said, "Listen, Peg, the most normal thing in the world is to react. When a person gets to the point when they can't react, they've got more troubles than a doctor can handle. But if you're going over to Buckner in the pickup tomorrow, you'd better eat hearty tonight."

He went back to eating, and she sat across staring at him. He was not a man of great depth. At least she had never thought of him as that kind of person, but that last remark had shown something more than an acceptance of John Bellanger's death. It had shown a kind of philosophical adaptation to both life and death, and Peggy Wheaton would have bet her last hundred dollars that her brother had never in his entire life thought about anything beyond his next meal and the inventory at their store.

CHAPTER TWO

THE AIR was gusty, the day was grayish without
sunlight, the clouds were tattered with soiled,
torn edges, but there was very little traffic on
the road between Brunswick and Buckner, and
that allowed her to look at the fields, the
farmhouses with gray tendrils rising from
fireplace chimneys, and the animals grazing
midst wheat stubble, impervious and fatalistic.

She had made this trip more times than she
could remember: as a small child, as a not-so-
small child, and now as a woman. She had
always liked it, for some obscure reason. She
still liked it. She had always liked rural things,
the unencumbered wind, the free-soaring leaves,
the rebirth each springtime. She had some
vague feeling about women being more capable
of really appreciating the four-season cycle of
nature than men could. But she had never
really tried to pin that down, to analyze it, and
she did not try now.

She reached Buckner an hour before noon,
which had been the plan because the men at the

railroad depot went to lunch from twelve until one o'clock and she'd had to wait a few times. She knew Dennis Mattingly, the assistant depot agent. They had in fact gone together for a couple of months during their last year in high school. Dennis not only found the boxes, he personally loaded them into the pickup for her, and as a final flourish, he invited her to stay over and have lunch with him down at Norma's cafe.

She begged off and drove out of town toward home, with that same long stretch of gunmetal road ahead. One advantage about this kind of a day was that there was no sun glare. The pickup had a heater. She was quite comfortable. There was also a radio in the truck, but she left it alone.

About six or seven miles out she saw what looked to her like a lanky, elderly farm woman wearing a rusty, unpressed long black dress and trying to change a tire at the side of the road. The elderly farm woman was bent forward, struggling with a bumper jack.

Margaret eased down, pulled off to the shoulder of the road, left the truck, and walked on up to see what help she could offer.

The heavy woman in the old black dress straightened up and turned—and it was a strikingly handsome man with sunburned blond hair, tanned features, and merry blue eyes. Margaret held her breath for two seconds. He was a minister of some kind; a priest or something like that.

He gazed at her quite soberly for a moment, then he laughed, and his entire handsome face lit up with whatever deep-down amusement had made him react like that.

"You look as though someone had just doused you with a bucketful of icewater," he said.

She smiled finally. "They did. I saw you as I was driving, and from back a few hundred yards I thought . . ."

He smiled a little more broadly. "You know, I've had this happen a dozen times before. You thought I was some poor helpless old woman who wouldn't know what to do, so you stopped to help."

Margaret nodded.

He studied her for a moment, and then he pointed to the handle of the bumper jack. "Fine. Just start working that thing up and down while I get the hubcap off and loosen the wheel lugs." He did not look at her again.

She worked the jack handle, he loosened the wheel, she raised the rear of the car a few more inches, he removed the flat tire, worked the spare into place, set two lugs by hand, and then nodded at her. "Let it down now."

She obeyed.

He was tightening the lugs when he finally looked directly at her again. "What's your name?" he asked.

"Margaret Wheaton. I'm from Brunswick. My brother and I own the general store in Brunswick."

He digested that while tightening down the

last lug. As he arose to push the flat tire to the trunk and toss it in, he said, "I'm Bill Tappan. I used to live in Buckner, but that was a long while ago. Lately, I've been in the army."

She had a peculiar feeling that something here did not fit; something was almost totally at variance between Bill Tappan and his ground-length black robe. She said, "You're *Father* Tappan, then?"

He rummaged in the trunk for a rag and cleaned his hands before he replied. "No. I'm not even a minister let alone a priest. I was an acolyte by appointment while I was in the service." He finished with the rag, handed it to her, and finished disengaging the jack while she dusted her own hands. He moved incisively, purposefully. He had everything in the trunk and had closed it down before she'd finished with the rag.

"A friend I was in the service with died up at Morriston last week. I came up because that was one of his requests, to assist in the graveyard ceremony." Tappan leaned and looked at her. "I was due in Brunswick at two o'clock this afternoon, so I had no time, really, after the burial back in Buckner, to change."

He smiled again. "Does that set it all to rights for you, Margaret?" His eyes twinkled merrily. "And you wouldn't have stopped if I had changed back in Buckner, would you?"

She laughed because although it was an unusual occurrence, at least now it was understandable. "No. Not if I'd just seen a large man with a flat tire."

He looked at his wrist. "I'm not going to make that appointment in Brunswick by two o'clock either." He stood gazing at her, friendly and absolutely relaxed, as though he didn't have an appointment anywhere, as though he was perfectly willing to stand there, loose and comfortable with her, throughout all eternity.

She said, "You could still *almost* make it if you hurried."

He shook his head. "That spare tire is slick. I've always privately thought that people who drive fast on treadless tires are fools. I don't want anyone to say that about me."

As she handed back the rag, he asked about Brunswick. All she could tell him was that he would see it for himself in another twenty-two or twenty-three miles, that it was a town with a population of about one thousand within the city limits and perhaps as many as another two or three thousand out in the countryside, that it had a rather stable, un-affluent economy, was delightful in summertime and she even liked it in wintertime.

She ended up by saying, "Massachusetts is the best part of all New England, Mr. Tappan," and for the first time his keen, alert blue eyes clouded over a little.

"What do you know of Vermont?" he asked, and she immediately sensed her error.

With a twinkle, she said, "Massachusetts is

the best part of New England . . . after Vermont?"

He laughed, and his gaze at her was full of strong approval. "I think I'll stay over a few days in Brunswick," he said.

That was her cue and she knew it, so she turned to go back to the truck. He waited until she had moved off a little ways, then he called after her.

"I have a cousin up in Burlington named Margaret. But they call her Peggy."

Margaret turned at the door of the truck. She knew exactly how she was supposed to answer. Instead, she simply smiled very sweetly, said, "Do they?" got into the truck, switched on the ignition, and as she eased back onto the pavement, threw him a little casual wave.

She did not see him again, but about five or six miles closer to Brunswick she saw his car in her rear-view mirror.

He passed her, eventually, on the outskirts of Brunswick, and where she had to turn up the rear alley to bring the truck to the dock out back of the store, she almost stopped thinking about him. Almost; there were two unusual elements in their meeting. One, of course, had been that long black dress, or gown, or whatever it was called, and the other was that she was sure he would wander into the store in the next day or two. Of course, she'd be at home. She only went down to the store occasionally.

But she had a premonition. They would meet again.

Earl came out to the dock, took the invoices

from her, and asked how the trip was. Uneventful, she told him, adding that *this* time she hadn't run out of gas.

He started unloading the boxes from the truck, and she checked to make certain they were all there. When Earl was finished, he straightened up with both hands pressed to his back, grimaced, and then looked at his watch.

"You made very good time," he said, sounding a little surprised.

She was mildly puzzled. "Was there some reason why I should have taken longer."

"No. Not exactly. I talked to Dennis on the telephone this morning. He mentioned something about taking you to lunch."

So *that* was it. She took the invoices from him and read through them as she'd done over at Buckner on the railroad platform, but over there she'd paid most attention to the number of cartons, not particularly their contents.

"Two dozen cotton dresses," she read, and looked up.

Earl gave her a little-boy smile. "Well, it's a new line and . . ."

"You don't buy women's dresses by the dozen, Earl, the way you buy two dozen boxes of nails or two dozen gate hinges."

He continued to smile, but he pursed his lips a little. He'd been running the store for a number of years now, and it had done very well; better, in fact, than it had under either of their parents. Of course, he did not come out on *everything* he bought, but he never really expected to. As for those dresses. . . .

"For the price, they'll sell," he replied. "And don't downgrade the merchandise until you've seen it. Come along inside. We'll let Morris bring the stuff inside and open the boxes."

He held the door for her; then he suddenly looked twice as she passed through. "Did you have car trouble?" he asked.

She shook her head before she understood that he'd seen her hands. "Well, I stopped to help—someone—change a flat tire."

His face cleared at once. "Oh. Someone from town?"

"Well, no, not exactly. A man in a long black . . ."

They were inside the big old barn of a store, with its shelves over shelves and its old-fashioned glass-front oak display cases. Nothing had changed inside, very much, since her father's day.

Earl paused beside the bolt goods counter. "A *man* wearing a *what*?"

She made a little fluttery gesture with both hands. "I thought it was a woman, so I stopped. It was a tall, blond man."

Earl stared. "In what?"

"Well, I thought at first he was a priest."

"Oh," Earl's face cleared instantly.

"But he wasn't a priest."

Earl's face slowly clouded again.

Margaret glanced at the invoices she was still holding. "He'd been to a friend's funeral over at Buckner. In the army he was an acolyte, and for some reason his friend wanted him at the churchyard ceremony in that same capacity. Afterward he had a two-o'clock appointment over here in Brunswick, and he didn't think he had the time to change, so that's how he happened to look like an old woman in a black dress when I . . ." She looked up. Earl was scratching his chin.

She said, "I'm starved. Would you like to take me up to the cafe for lunch?"

Earl nodded and took the invoices to the cubbyhole office in the back of the building, and she heard him talking to Morris back there about the cartons on the dock.

She laughed to herself. It *had* sounded pretty darned improbable.

She strolled toward the front of the old building and stopped at the door, waiting. The smell in the store had always intrigued her, even when she'd been a small child. It was part oil from the ancient floor, part faint flower fragrance from the soap and sundry counter, and part a lot of other things that she'd never been able to pin down. But it was pleasant, in an old-fashioned kind of way.

CHAPTER THREE

SOME PEOPLE never put much faith in premonitions. Margaret Wheaton didn't either, as a rule. She was out front swearing under her breath at a recalcitrant storm window, something her brother was supposed to install all around the house each late autumn and never did, when she heard the scuff of leather over wood and twisted to look over her shoulder.

He was coming up the stairs, and she hadn't even heard him turn in off the sidewalk out front. Perhaps that was because there was a slight wind blowing, and perhaps it was also because she had been concentrating so hard on the darned storm window, which simply refused to fit into place.

He moved up behind her, reached around her, and took the window in both powerful hands. She released it, ducked down, and stepped away. Neither of them had spoken a word. They did not speak now. She watched his wide mouth flatten, his strong arms straighten, as he changed the position of the storm window slightly, then heaved his weight against it. The window grated solidly into place.

Then he turned and said, "Good morning."

He was wearing brown corduroy trousers, a gray turtleneck sweater, and an old tweed jacket. He didn't even look the same in the face for some reason. Now, he looked like—well—just a very handsome man who spent a lot of time out of doors.

She looked ruefully at the problem window as she answered him. "Good morning. I've been fighting that window for fifteen minutes."

He turned back toward the window. "You ought to stick to what you know, Peg, like making meatloaf."

She stared. "What?"

"Meatloaf," he said, and laughed.

"Who've you been talking to, Mr. Tappan?"

He ran an experienced hand around the edges of the storm window. "Your brother. In fact we had coffee across the road at the cafe a little while ago."

She was puzzled. Earl wasn't the kind of man who . . . "How did my brother happen to mention my meatloaf, Mr. Tappan?"

He leaned on the front of the house, with wind ruffling his short, taffy-colored hair. "We talked about a whole range of subjects, and somewhere along the line he mentioned that old John Bellanger used to drop round for dinner whenever he thought you might be baking a meatloaf. Your brother told me you made the finest, most exotic meatloaf in all of Massachusetts. Now, what interests me, Peg, is whether you could qualify as the best meatloafer in Vermont as well."

She couldn't hold back the twinkle. "An *exotic* meatloaf?"

He laughed, and that made her laugh too. Then he said, "I'm a lawyer. My office is up at Burlington in Vermont. If you hadn't been in such a hurry yesterday, I'd have asked you another question: where the John Bellanger residence was. This morning your brother told me. That's how we happened to go have coffee together. I represent a distant cousin of John Bellanger. He couldn't drive down himself so he asked me to."

Margaret thought of the little white-trimmed brown house at the far end of Elm Street. John Bellanger had always kept it so neat; every gate worked, each slat in the fence was replaced the moment it broke. The leaves were never allowed to lie unraked on the lawn out front, and there had been the garden and the rose bed out back. It had always seemed to Margaret Wheaton like an oversized residence of elves or some kind of little happy beings. Once, John Bellanger had made a rope-swing for her, when she'd been no more than nine, from below the immense old apple tree out back.

"What will happen to his house, now?" she asked.

Tappan, watching her face, said, "I understand he was a friend of your father and mother years ago. Your brother told me you took broken toys up to him."

Margaret nodded. "He was special, Mr. Tappan. My father died when I was almost too young to know him. John Bellanger substituted, over the years."

The handsome, tall man understood. "I had an uncle like that. Well, about the house—I'm to look it over and see about selling it." His gaze drifted away, then back again. "That might take a few days. What his heir is worried about is having it vacant; vandalism and so forth, you understand."

She scoffed at that. "Not in Brunswick, Mr. Tappan. The last case like that was last halloween when some high-school boys took the cross off the church steeple and nailed it on top of Jim Burley's garage. In Brunswick we don't even have any worthwhile demonstrators. Last year four college students held a car race just outside town, and Jim Burley's brother, who is our police officer, locked them up, and Jim, who is also the justice of the peace, fined each one a hundred dollars. That went for new books at the school library."

He smiled at her. "Sounds so peaceful it must be dreary."

She looked at him after he said that; somewhere inside her his last word fell like glass and shattered into a hundred pieces. Was *that* it; was that what had been troubling her this past year when she'd felt restless, purposeless, sometimes a little at war with herself or with *something* anyway?

She covered her silence by offering him coffee, but he refused. "I had two cups with your brother. That's enough to last me until tomorrow." He turned and looked beyond the leafless big trees and the rooftops where the mountains curved round from west to north, far off across the autumn countryside. "Good skiing up here later on?"

There was. In fact, a couple of years ago a New York development company had scouted the hills beyond Brunswick, so it was rumored all over town, with some idea of perhaps building a ski resort in the distant foothills. Nothing had ever come of that, though.

"Good enough, I suppose," she replied. "Now and then we get people over from Boston or from some other city. But there won't be enough snow for skiing for another month or six weeks and maybe not even then. We don't always get an early snow." She thought of something. "But there's Miller's pond, west of town four miles. That's where I learned to ice skate."

"Okay," he said, turning back toward her. "When do you want to go out there?"

She gave him her sweetest smile. "We haven't had enough freezing weather yet. I'm sorry."

"Well, then, suppose we just went driving in the countryside. It's beautiful around Brunswick. I'd like to see it all."

She kept on smiling at him. "Just drive, Mr. Tappan, you don't need a guide. Every road you'll take out of Brunswick will eventually

bring you back again. Now, I've still got four
more storm windows to put up."

He straightened up and rubbed his hands
together. "If they all fit like that last one did,
you're not going to be able to put them up by
yourself."

That, she thought, was probably very true.
But she did not want to be with him any more.
It wasn't that he was so confident; she didn't
really know what it was, but it was *something*.
Yesterday had been fun, in its own harmless
way. Today they were hitting it off *too* well.

But he went over where the storm windows
were leaning, selected one, took it to the far
front window and stood like a portrait painter,
scowling from the storm window to the sill. She
sighed. "There's a number on the top of each
one. There is a corresponding number on each
sill on the left side. My brother did that a few
years ago because he could never remember
which window fit which frame. What number is
on the window?"

He looked. "Three."

She knew that was wrong because her brother
had started the numbering from the left side of
the building. "It should be two."

They spent two hours at it and finally got
each storm window in place. In some ways he
reminded her of Earl. In other ways he was
completely different; he stopped several times
as they were working down the north side of the
house and looked off toward the westerly moun-

tains. He just looked, he didn't say anything, but she got the feeling that he liked mountains, that he probably liked anything that had to do with the out-of-doors.

When they finished, she took him to the pantry where there was a sink, and he washed his hands. Then she offered to feed him, but he shook his head and teased her. "Not even if it's some of your meatloaf. But there's one thing you could do for me?"

She turned chary. "Possibly."

"Okay. When you thank me for helping with the windows, call me Bill."

She almost laughed at him. "Thank you, Bill."

He went back to the door. "It was as easy as falling off a log, wasn't it?" he said, and stepped back outside. "I enjoyed it, Peg. Goodbye."

She stood a moment wanting to go after him and thank him properly. She also did *not* want to go after him, whatever the reason.

Finally, she went through to the front of the house, but he had already disappeared in the direction of the business area of town.

She went to her room, showered, changed, and went out to the kitchen. It was getting dark out already and it was just barely four o'clock. Usually, in autumn the days darkened early but not *this* early.

She started dinner and only glanced at the wall barometer by accident on her way to the pantry for a jar of pickles. The red hand was stationary, as it usually was, but the spidery black hand with its little arrowhead-pointer was about as far down as it could go without leaving the area marked "stormy."

She went to the window and leaned, looking outward and upward. It was too early for a real storm, but of course there was one thing you could count upon with Mother Nature: just when you knew what she would do, she did exactly the opposite.

It didn't matter. She went back to work and when Earl came in later, complaining that his back was bothering him, she made a strong highball and took it to him in the living room where he'd dropped into a chair to read the *Enterprise,* something he did almost every night before dinner. It was, actually, about the only time of the day he got a chance to sit down to read.

Later, when he came out to eat, he looked a lot better. She was glad because she had something to tell him. As they sat down to eat, she let him have both barrels.

"Will you please explain to me why you had to tell a complete stranger I make good meatloaf?"

He looked up with his mouth full, blinked, chewed a moment, then said, "You mean Bill Tappan? Where did you meet him?"

"This afternoon he helped me put up the darned storm windows that you never find the time to put up."

He swallowed and looked at her again, longer this time. She usually had a very nice disposition. Of course, not always, but usually. She also had a priceless sense of humor. He liked her, not because she was his sister but just because he liked her kind of person.

"I'd have put those windows up next Sunday," he said defensively.

She did not argue. She knew exactly what he was doing; leading the conversation away from her question. "Why did you have to mention the meatloaf, Earl?"

"Well. He—that is, we,—got to talking about John Bellanger, and I just happened to mention how he used to like to come over when you made meatloaf. It was a perfectly harmless thing to say, Peg."

"And you told him people called me Peggy."

He looked more and more baffled. "What's so terrible about that? That's what folks *do* call you?"

She suddenly heard herself. She sounded like someone else, sounded shrewish and nagging. She leaped up. "Finish your coffee and I'll get you some more."

Earl drained the cup, put it down very gently, and stared after her as she went to the sideboard. "What the hell," he muttered under his breath, "has got into her?"

She didn't hear it so she didn't have to answer. If she *could* have answered!

CHAPTER FOUR

IT STORMED that night, exactly as the kitchen barometer had predicted, but Peggy Wheaton did not know it and neither did her brother until they awakened the following morning. The reason they did not know it was simply because the falling snow did not make a sound.

When Peggy arose, the entire world beyond her windows was white. She went to look out. It hadn't just been a snow*fall*, it had been a snow*storm*. She hastened to shower and dress and head for the kitchen. For some reason that probably had to do with her prehistoric ancestors, whenever there was this kind of a serious storm, she felt impelled to move more briskly than usual and to start cooking hot food.

By the time Earl appeared, wearing a heavy sweater over his woolen shirt, she had hot coffee, oatmeal, and hot toast waiting. He shook his head at her. "Business will be lousy today. It always is when a big one comes." He sat down. "I can't remember when we got one *this* early though, can you?"

She couldn't, but since she'd already decided that, she simply said, "It's too early, Earl. We'll have a thaw tomorrow and probably sunshine."

He pointed to the barometer with the piece of toast he was holding. The barometer had not moved from where it had been yesterday.

Later, after her brother was gone and she had gone over the house lightly, giving tabletops and shelves a lick and a promise more than a dusting, she put on a pair of heavy slacks, a red plaid shirt, a scarf, and her quilted jacket and went out front to the porch.

The air was keen and absolutely still. It was not as cold as one might have expected. The clouds were low and scarcely moving. Off in the direction of the mountains, virgin whiteness stretched all the way to the spike-topped tiers of dark pines. Nearer, down at the curb where a pair of huge old trees stood, a few forlorn, withered brown leaves still clung doggedly to some naked limbs despite their weight of snow.

It was a transformed, beautifully clean and silent world. She went down as far as the sidewalk by following her brother's tracks. He hadn't even tried taking the car out, which was just as well since there was a white drift two feet high against the garage doors.

School was closed, evidently, because she began seeing youngsters dragging sleds toward the little hills beyond town as she mushed her way in the direction of Brunswick's business district. No one had tried to drive down the street yet, and until she was within shouting

distance of the stores along Main Street, she
didn't see a single car being driven. No one, in a
place with such short distances as Brunswick
had, put on tire chains if they could avoid it, if
they could walk where they had to go, or if they
could persuade themselves they didn't have to
go anywhere and stayed home to stoke the
fireplace.

It was one of those mornings that made a
person feel freshly arrived in a new world. She
had always thrilled to the first snowfall. In fact,
she had always thrilled to each first sign of the
change of seasons. She met Harriett Stokes,
whose father owned the drug store. They had
attended school together. Harriett was wearing
a fur cap that made her look like some kind of
half-girl, half-animal, and her hazel eyes beamed
pleasure in all directions as she clomped in
beside Peggy, taking clumsy steps in her boots,
and said, "Remember when we used to head for
the slopes west of town with my brother's
toboggan?"

Peggy remembered. They'd had to pull the
darned toboggan, which seemed to weigh a ton
in those days, to the top of a small hill, then
they raced downward and in moments were
right back where they had to struggle to get the
taboggan back up again. Later, it had seemed to
Peggy to be an awful lot of work for the fleeting
thrill.

"I remember getting soaked to the skin," she
said, laughing. "And I remember the boys throwing snowballs at us as we raced down the hill."

Harriett had matured into a muscular, robust woman, a little shorter than average. She had been married for four years to a traveling salesman she'd met at an Independence Day celebration. They had parted only last year, and Harriett now worked in her father's drug store.

His name was John Varnum; he was a quiet, smiling man, and Harriett had his hazel eyes and dark hair, but she was exuberant, bubbly, full of life, and in years past before life and a divorce had matured her, Harriett had been one of those very effervescent, very healthy people who couldn't cram all the living they had to do into any one day.

Now, Harriett said, "What would people say if we went and dug out the old toboggan and dragged it up there west of town?"

Peggy laughed at the picture of them, both grown women now, doing that. "They'd probably say we were in our second childhood."

For Harriett, the thought was kin to the deed. "Are you game?" she said, stopping suddenly and facing Peggy.

For a moment Peggy was willing, then she saw someone crossing the street in their direction, and for as long as it took her to recognize him and to think about him, she said nothing. Harriett followed out the line of Peggy's gaze, saw the handsome, tall man with the taffy-hair coming toward them, and almost asked who he was, but a small inhibition stopped her; she also saw something in Peggy Wheaton's face that kept her silent.

Bill Tappan was dressed for the weather. He looked happy, too, as though this sort of thing delighted him. When he stepped onto the curb, Peggy introduced him to Harriett Varnum Stokes—and noticed the slight widening of Harriett's large hazel eyes, the slight, lilting lift to the far corners of her lips, when she responded to the introduction.

"It's wonderful," he said, raising his arms slightly as though to indicate everything in sight. "In Vermont we don't usually get one this early. Usually not much before Thanksgiving Day." His eyes lit on Peggy's rosy face and stayed there. "If I had a sled, I'd take you riding."

Harriett jumped in. "That's what we were talking about, Mr. Tappan; about when we were kids how we used to take my brother's toboggan to the hills west of town and spend entire days dragging that thing around."

Harriett, true to type, then said, "It's better than a sled. It will hold three adults or six kids." The hazel eyes clung to Bill Tappan's face. "Are you game, Mr. Tappan?"

Peggy began to feel uncomfortable for some reason. Not just because they were all well past the age for this sort of thing, but for some other, less definable reason. She hoped he would refuse and was sure he would; Harriett had always had some pretty hairbrained spur-of-the-moment ideas.

But he didn't refuse. "I'm game, Mrs. Stokes. How far do we have to drag the toboggan?"

Harriett turned without another word of explanation. "Come along then," she said, "follow me."

Bill Tappan looked at Peggy. She decided to make an excuse and go across the road to the general store. He reached and took her arm and steered her along in Harriett's wake, and she allowed herself to be taken along.

The old Varnum house where Harriett and her father lived now—her brother was an aerospace executive out in California and had been for six or seven years—was on the back street that held most of the newer residences. Behind it was open country all the way to the westerly hills. Of course, it belonged to someone; in fact, this particular land belonged to Harriett's uncle, her father's brother, who farmed both west and north of town.

They went directly to a large combination tool and storage shed, and Harriett plunged through the accumulated castoffs like a curvy little hazel-eyed bear seeking a honeycomb. Bill Tappan laughed at her and then stepped over to help. They worked the dusty toboggan free, carried it outside, and when Bill put it down on the snow, it began to glide almost as though it possessed a mind of its own.

Harriett closed the storeroom door and beamed. "It still works," she exclaimed.

They took it about a half-mile out, where the first small, round hill was. Bill Tappan ploughed his way to the top without even breathing hard; then he set the toboggan in place, aimed it, and told Harriett to sit up front. She got into place. Peggy got behind her, and it did not occur to her that there might have been a plan to this arrangement until Bill eased down behind her.

He called, "Ready?" Harriett squealed and Bill pushed off. Then he leaned very close, slid both arms round Peggy's middle, and held on that way.

The old toboggan fairly flew. There was more than enough snow to support their combined weight, but what made it even better was the hard crust on top of the snowpack.

Harriett squealed again, and even Peggy laughed as cold air made her squint her eyes almost closed. They had the weight and the slope to build up a surprising momentum. The only way they could steer the toboggan was by leaning, all together. Bill's arms, hugging Peggy, drew her sideward. She leaned. Harriett felt the change of course and also leaned. They made a huge, speeding half circle, which carried them close to the nearest back street, and then they gradually began to lose headway, finally stopping.

Harriett jumped up, breathless and excited. She hardly gave Bill a chance to catch the rope and start dragging the toboggan back toward their hill again. "That was the best ride I *ever* had," she exclaimed, panting so hard that steam rose with each word. "The snow is just exactly right."

Peggy laughed at her exuberance; this was the Harriett she had grown up with, so full of life and energy she couldn't stand still.

They returned to the top of the little hill, and on that second trip down, because the snow had been packed by their first trip, they went even faster and farther. Bill clung tightly to Peggy. She leaned back a little when they made their big curve at the end of the run, and with his lips close to her ear, he said, "I wish I'd found you five years ago."

Then the ride ended, Harriett rolled off the toboggan into the snow, they laughed at her, and the process was repeated again for the third time. But that time, Harriett and Peggy changed places, and that time Bill did not sit, legs on either side as they sped away. Instead, he knelt behind Harriett, holding to the side-ropes, and when it was time to turn, he leaned with all his weight to make a sharper turn—the rotten old rope broke, and Bill Tappan ploughed up six feet of loose snow with his head and arms.

The toboggan sank deeply on one side, then careened sideward and dumped its last two passengers. The last view the girls had of Bill was with his head buried, his feet in the air, throwing up a regular cloud of snow. They sat up to their waists in snow, laughing. When he rolled over and sat up digging snow from his face, they had to laugh even harder. Peggy gasped, finally, and got to her feet. The snow was melting from body heat, the way it had when she'd been a child. In those days the cold had been much less noticeable than it was now.

Bill stood up and shook like a bear. He grinned at his own appearance, and the three of them started across the short distance toward the back of the Varnum place, panting, wet, cold, and laughing.

They saw some children gravely watching from a nearby yard, and waved. One child waved back, but not too enthusiastically; perhaps the adults had taken over their sliding hill.

At Harriett's house they put away the toboggan. She wanted them to come in and dry out, but Peggy begged-off. She wanted to get home. Bill Tappan made an excuse; he had to meet someone over on Elm Street in about an hour, and it would take him that long to shower and change and look properly dignified again.

They parted, and Peggy went home hardly aware of the condition of her clothing, of her hair. She did not even see how people looked around as she trudged past them. All she thought of was how much fun that had been and how easy it had been for her to forget a lot of sobering things, at least for a couple of hours.

CHAPTER FIVE

PEGGY HAD been wrong in her prediction at the breakfast table: the sun did not come out and there was no overnight thaw. On the contrary, although the sky finally cleared, it did so during the night, and by morning there were glass-like ice crystals everywhere, even in the trees.

Earl agreed that it was beautiful, but when Peggy said it was like a fairyland, that was a bit much. "Fairies don't buy much at the store," he said, and finished breakfast with a grin when his sister looked disgustedly at him. "Okay, it's absolutely ecstatic. By the way, yesterday afternoon I heard some little kids complaining about grown people ruining their sled-run west of town. One of them was Jim Burley's kid."

Earl rose and shrugged into his heavy jacket. Peggy was clearing the table when she commented on the episode with Harriett Stokes and Bill Tappan. "I'm sure that's all you heard," she said dryly, and Earl looked at her from the doorway.

40

"As a matter of fact, it wasn't."

She raised her eyes to him. "I'll make application to the nearest convent today."

He hung there a moment, then winked at her and turned to leave the house. Ordinarily he would have said something more, but over the past couple of days he had felt some small warnings and had begun to heed them. He had never married, and this was one of the reasons; women were just too murky, and there were so many other things in life that *weren't* murky.

Peggy was finishing the dishes when the telephone rang. It was Harriett Stokes still breathless over the fun they'd had the previous day. She also said she'd found out who Bill Tappan was and proceeded to tell Peggy that Bill was the lawyer for old John Bellanger's small estate, or something like that, which, for Harriett, was very good; usually she did not get that close to the facts.

She also told Peggy he was the most delightful man she'd met in ages. Peggy neither agreed nor disagreed. That first day, back along the highway between Brunswick and Buckner, when they'd first met, she had thought Bill Tappan was very handsome; she probably still thought so although she was not so sure now because he had projected more than just his appearance into her life. He had projected his personality, and yesterday on the toboggan he had whispered something in her ear that had been more personal than she wanted him, or any other man, to be with her.

Still, for the sake of conversation, she agreed with Harriett. It cost nothing and if she'd hesitated or had disagreed, Harriett would have probed for her reasons, and that would have gotten Peggy even more involved.

Then Harriett seemed to brush Bill Tappan aside. She said, "The ice is six inches thick up at Miller's pond. If I come by for you in an hour, will you go up there skating with me?"

Peggy was willing. She was not only a good skater, but she thoroughly enjoyed doing it. "Sure. It'll take me an hour to hunt up my skates and get dressed." She had a sudden thought. "You'd better have chains put on your car at Burley's garage, Harriett. That road's four miles of icy slush by now."

Harriett said, "Don't stew," and hung up.

Peggy's spirits rose steadily as she rummaged in a low pantry drawer and found her skates; then she went to bundle into warm clothing. She made a Thermos of hot coffee and a little packet of beef sandwiches. Skating made people hungry, and Miller's pond was a long way from the cafe in town.

She heard Harriett drive up in front, tire chains clanking over the icy roadway like tank treads. She grabbed the Thermos, the sandwiches, her skates, which she slung over one shoulder, made sure the mittens and knitted cap were in her pockets, and ran out of the house. She was halfway to the car before she remembered that she'd brought no matches. She did not turn back. There probably would be other skaters up at Miller's pond today; someone would have the means for starting a driftwood-fire.

Harriett beamed at the sandwiches and Thermos. "I never thought of that," she said, heading away from the curb.

Peggy agreed. "You never did years back, either."

Harriett smiled. "I didn't have to. You were always the level-headed, very practical member of our duo. By the way, my dad heard about us ploughing up all that snow yesterday. He was interested in your boyfriend."

That took the wind out of Peggy's sails. "My—what? I don't know him any better than you do."

Harriett turned her large hazel eyes. "All right. I'm not deaf. I only know that *you* introduced him to *me*. That boyfriend thing was just a figure of speech." The hazel eyes lingered upon Peggy. When they finally went back to the road, Harriett was subdued and thoughtful for about a mile, until they left the main road and struck out due west on a country lane lined with large, barren sycamore trees that looked, now, like crooked dark veins pushing upward toward the steel sky.

"We're not the first," said Peggy.

There were car tracks all the way, but after studying them for the first mile and a half, they decided that it was no more than two cars. But, of course, that could mean more than two couples. The only way to be certain was to drive on up and see.

They did not discuss the episode in the snow again; in fact, Harriett had had her warning, and she did not elude to Bill Tappan again either. She talked about Earl, though, and very gradually, as they slid and clanked and ploughed their way along, Peggy began to suspect that there was something more to her friend's tone of voice than just simple conversational interest.

It was preposterous, of course. Harriett and Earl were eons apart in every way that mattered. Moreover, Earl was almost thirty, and even if he hadn't said at least a dozen times that Peggy could remember that he would never marry, he was so well entrenched in his habits that she couldn't conceive of him ever changing.

Then they saw the lake, saw the skaters out upon it. "A dozen," said Peggy. "That's not bad."

She was right because Miller's pond, which had been named after the farming family which owned both the lake itself and all the land around it for a long distance in all directions, was not less than a hundred acres in size. It was actually a lake fed by an underground spring, but it had always been called Miller's pond as far back as anyone could remember.

Harriett parked the car beside two other vehicles, near the lakeshore, and as she and Peggy went ahead and sat on the snow to put on their skates, two teenagers skimmed past. The girl was one of the numerous Burley brood. She smiled with beautiful teeth and waved. They waved back. The boy was a stranger to Peggy.

Harriett said, "With animals, mating season is in the spring. With humans, it's any time. Come on, let's try the ice."

Peggy was accustomed to Harriett's earthy comments. She nevertheless looked up disapprovingly this time, but Harriett was already making her way gingerly out upon the ice. Harriett looked back and said, "I'll be darned; it'll hold me up."

The other skaters were far away. The air was clear and the nearby mountain slopes were like a painting on new canvas. Peggy made a few runs; then, her confidence returning in a rush, she returned to where Harriett was kneeling, making an adjustment to her right skate. Without looking up, Harriett said, "He's not my shadow, so he must be yours."

Peggy had to decode that first; then she twisted and slowly looked out over the lake. *There he was!*

She watched him, surprised and also annoyed. But of course he had as much right to be there as anyone else. In fact—and now she remembered doing it—she was the one who had told him about Miller's pond.

He was an accomplished skater. He had the ideal build for it, and he had something else that went a long way toward making skaters graceful: perfect poise and coordination.

He was out a ways. As Harriett stood up and tested the adjusted skate, she said, "We're going to bump into him sooner or later, you know."

Peggy did not answer that. She simply said, "Let's go up to the other end; that's where the driftwood usually piles up."

They skated swiftly, and because Peggy was leading, they stayed close to the south shoreline. Harriett, who was powerful on skates, looked back a couple of times. When they got to the farthest shore, she looked back one more time. Bill Tappan had skated over to where they had been, near the south shore, and was making a leisurely sweep in their direction. Harriett, for once, did not shoot from the hip; she said nothing and went back and forth with Peggy Wheaton, gathering snow-soggy dead wood for their fire.

When they had enough, Harriett looked at the pile and held out a mittened hand. Peggy sighed. "I don't have any."

Harriett dropped her hand. "Neither do I. *He* does. I'd bet money on it."

Peggy turned. Bill Tappan was sweeping closer but without haste, and once he swerved far wide and rode a virgin stretch of ice almost to the middle of the pond before making a wide, graceful curve heading directly for them.

Harriett said, "I wonder what he *can't* do well, Peg?"

She got no reply.

Bill was wearing a white-knit, bulky turtleneck sweater under a plaid jacket when he coasted up and called out a greeting to them. They answered, in two different tones. Then Harriett, pointing to their small pile of wood, asked if he had any matches. He did have. He hardly looked at Peggy as he went past, knelt, and went to work trying to coax a fire out of some half-dry pine needles. It took a lot of effort, but eventually he got a pencil-thin finger of flame started, and as he looked upward, Harriett said, "You must have been a Boy Scout."

He got back on his feet. "What's my reward; a cup of coffee?"

Peggy looked sharply at him. He must have seen them arrive, must have seen her place the Thermos beside the hood of the car, which her brother had taught her to do. He certainly had a knack for dropping harmless little verbal bombs. Yesterday it had been what he had whispered in her ear. The day before that it had been his remark about her meatloaf. Today, the coffee.

Harriett was gazing past him at Peggy when she said, "Let's wait and see if it really burns." Then she pushed off with a powerful glide. The ice at this end of the pond was smoother. As though they were still in their teens, Harriett called back, "Follow the leader!"

Peggy, who had always been fast and graceful on skates, swung in behind Harriett. Within moments Bill Tappan was beside her. He seemed able to anticipate everything she did. She tried a trick and he even anticipated that. She smiled and he smiled back. A dozen yards onward she raised one foot for a reversing pirouette. When she looked around, he was right there beside her, heading back the way they had come. This time they both laughed. Harriett, though, who had decided to turn on some speed, was flying off in the opposite direction, and that was funny too.

He offered Peggy a hand. She took it, crossed her other arm over, and they skated as a twosome for half the length of the pond before Harriett, almost at the far end, down where the cars were, stopped, looked back, and saw them. She pulled off her furry cap, flung it upon the ice, and both Peggy and Bill Tappan almost fell when they broke out laughing.

While Harriett was coming back, he said, "Quickly, before your friend gets here, tell me something: is there any other place in Brunswick to have dinner tonight than the hotel?"

There was, of course. "The restaurant directly across from the general store. That place where you and my brother had . . ." She let it trail off. He knew; of course he already knew that there was another place. She looked at him as he released her hands.

"All right," he said, veering off sharply. "I'll be by for you at seven o'clock." He was out of earshot within seconds, and when Harriett finally got back, Peggy was red in the face and sultry-eyed. But she did not say a word.

CHAPTER SIX

SHE TOLD herself, when they got back about dusk from Miller's pond, that she might have gone to dinner with him if he'd asked her honestly and candidly, but she most certainly would *not* go to dinner with him now, after he'd tricked her into suggesting the restaurant.

In fact, by the time Harriett dropped her off and she went into the house to bathe and change, she had made up her mind that she did not really like him, after all.

She had never liked bold, brassy boys, and now that she was a woman, that applied to men.

Earl arrived home early. He and Morris, he told her when they met in the living room, had decided it was costing more to keep the store open, with all the lights and the heat on, than they could possibly pick up in desultory sales, so they had locked up for the night.

After he told her this, he stood in front of the fireplace, gazing steadily at her. Her face was still flushed from the wind up at Miller's pond,

49

but there had to be more to it than that. After all, Earl had grown up with her, and in a sense he had been more parent than brother after the passing of their mother.

He started to say something, then checked himself up short. She knew him, too, possibly better than he knew her, so she finally said, "Harriett and I went skating up at Miller's pond today."

He nodded, beginning to look relieved.

"Bill Tappan was up there. He tricked me into going to dinner with him this evening."

She knew what Earl was going to say before he even opened his mouth. She was right; he said, "Tricked you? How does someone trick you into going to dinner with them, Peg?"

She didn't explain it; she simply said, "Earl, when he comes along, will you meet him at the door for me; will you tell him I'm not going with him tonight?"

Earl continued to stand before the cold fireplace, hands in pockets. Finally he said, "No."

She was surprised, although she probably shouldn't have been. Excluding a few violent brawls during her lifetime, he had consistently refused to bail her out.

Once, when she'd been going with Dennis Mattingly from over in Buckner and she'd wanted him to alibi for her, he had said, "Look, Peg, you're not a little kid any longer. You get yourself into these things. You get yourself out as well."

She knew, if she pressed the issue tonight,

he'd say about the same thing. She turned and
went out to the kitchen, and about fifteen
minutes later, when he'd finished the newspaper,
he sauntered out, silently made them two
highballs, silently set hers beside her elbow at
the sink, and silently took his over to the table
where he sat down.

Then he said, "Bill Tappan bought the Bellanger place himself, yesterday. John Varnum
told me. He got it straight from the notary over
in Buckner who recorded the deed."

Peggy had to think that over, so she continued
working for a while in silence, and in the
meanwhile her brother finished his highball.
Then he spoke again.

"He's a nice guy, Peg. I'm not trying to sell
him to you. I don't care, personally, whether
you like him or not. That's your business. But
he's a nice guy."

The doorbell rang and she turned, finally,
pale and dark-eyed. Earl slowly shook his head,
which meant he would not go answer it. She
dried her hands, touched her hair, and marched
resolutely out to the entry-way. She took a big
breath, reached for the knob, and opened the
door.

Something below her line of vision stirred, so
she dropped her eyes from Bill Tappan's face
into the sober, lifted round face of a big-eyed
little boy who was wearing a tie and a blue
sports coat and who looked up at her as though
he wasn't really sure what to expect. Then he
smiled, perhaps because what he saw he liked.

He was a handsome child, no more than four or five years old, but he was holding himself very erect and proper.

She smiled back in spite of herself. Bill Tappan, one step behind the child, said, "Miss Wheaton, this is Michael Harland Tappan. My son."

She felt the full weight of those last two words and looked up, startled. It was too late to hide the astonishment. She looked down again and Michael Harland Tappan offered her a small, scrubbed hand. Her heart melted all at once. She dropped down, took the hand, and gravely shook it. Then she said, "I'm very glad to meet you, Michael Harland Tappan."

The child's round eyes did not leave her face. He said, "Do you want to go to dinner with us . . . please?"

She looked at Bill. He said, "I only told him you *might* go to dinner with us."

Michael Harland Tappan clung to her hand. "If you do," he said, speaking slowly, "we could go now because I'm hungry."

She raised a hand to his light hair, pushed a lock into place, then rose, still with him holding her hand. "You come inside out of the cold," she told him, "and I'll go change, and we'll go to dinner. And I'll hurry because I'm hungry too."

Earl came from the kitchen at the sound of the door closing. He blinked at the child. Peggy introduced them as Earl came forward smiling. She looked over their heads at Bill Tappan.

He looked straight back with nothing bold or

brassy in his expression. She turned and ran out of the room.

Of course he had brought the child along deliberately, but what had stunned her in the doorway was that he had a child. That meant he also had a wife. She sank down at the dressing table. The child hadn't been with him when they'd met on the Buckner road.

She finally got up and started to dress, not because she wanted to go to dinner with Bill Tappan but because Michael Harland Tappan was hungry, and at four or five years of age there could be nothing more important than eating when one was hungry.

She put on a dark dress with light trim, did what she had to with her hair, looked at her flushed face in the mirror—and suddenly thought of the people she had known all her life in Brunswick who would see her eating in the restaurant with a man and a little boy.

But instead of making her despair, this somehow made her smile. Brunswick, she had known all her life, was a place where people took a very keen interest in the affairs of everyone else. Even Earl, who could not be a gossip without injuring his trade at the store, always managed to know things. Tonight, Margaret Wheaton would shock the heck out of them!

She returned to the living room. The men were talking, and someone had given Michael a cookie from the kitchen. He was dropping crumbs all down the front of his white shirt and his elegant little coat. She went over and helped him get rid of the crumbs, and when she turned her brother was holding a coat for her. Their eyes met, but Earl had been dealing with people for far too many years to show anything. But she knew he was laughing at her.

Outside, the night was as still as glass and almost as clear and brilliant. It was also cold. Bill had a car at the curb. As he helped her in, then placed his son between them on the front seat, he said, "I apologize."

She met his glance easily. "There is nothing to apologize about. I think he's beautiful."

"Not *him*. For doing that to you up at the lake today."

They turned and headed back down the icy street toward the center of town. Michael Harland Tappan leaned against her. He was warm, and although she was certain neither he nor his father would have liked to hear her say it, she thought he was also wonderfully soft.

When he pulled up in front of the store, directly across from the restaurant, she said, "Drive down in front of the hotel. The meals are much better."

He obeyed. As they left the car, Michael groped for her fingers. She removed a glove so that their hands could intertwine properly. She smiled and winked, and the little boy said. "I'm Mike."

She laughed at him. "I like that. Mike."

Inside, the first person she saw was Harriett Stokes having dinner with her father. Harriett looked speechless, which made Peggy smile across the crowded room at her, very sweetly.

It wasn't Saturday night, which was when most of Brunswick ate out, but it could have been. The hotel's diningroom was full. People looked up, some started, some simply nodded, and a few smiled at her as they were led to a corner table.

Bill Tappan held her chair; then he leaned down and said, "I couldn't leave him in my room upstairs."

She waited until he was seated opposite her before replying. "Of course you couldn't. And of course he just happened along today so you could bring him to my front door."

Bill leaned to place the napkin in his son's lap, and then he straightened back with a solemn look at her, and a sigh.

"As a matter of fact, his mother sent him to me down here, with a letter. Would you like to see it?"

She got a sinking sensation in the pit of her stomach. "*Sent* him to you?"

"Yes. Sent him on the train to Buckner in the care of a conductor."

Peggy stared. "A little boy like this . . . ?"

Bill reached inside his jacket and put an opened envelope in front of her. "Read it," he said, as the waitress arrived for their orders. She did not touch the envelope, and when Bill ordered for all three of them, she did not take her eyes off him. Afterward she said, "Do I have to know, Bill?"

He picked up the envelope and tucked it

away again. "No, you don't have to know. She left me. She's done it before. But you see, with Mike, I couldn't do what I should have done; what I really wanted to do. So I hung on. But this time she sent him down to me in Brunswick. This time she flew to Europe, and this time, Peg, she won't be back."

Their meal arrived. The waitress was very careful, and when she served the child, he looked up into her face the same way he'd looked up into Peggy's face, and smiled. His smile, Peggy thought, would melt stones. The waitress smiled back, then hovered over him a moment before departing.

Peggy hadn't been hungry before. Now she couldn't even make the effort, but when Mike asked why she didn't eat, she had to try.

She looked mutely at Bill. He smiled crookedly back. There really was nothing more to be said. Certainly not in front of the child. They probably already had said too much, but if Michael Harland Tappan had any problems, they certainly did not appear to impair his appetite.

Peggy used his napkin for him twice, and after the last time when he said, very gravely, "Thank you," she had to struggle to hold it back, but she managed.

She watched the child, marveling that any woman could have deliberately put him on a train to a town she probably wasn't even certain existed, send him to a man who might not even be at that town, pay his fare one way, and then turn her back on him and fly to the other side of the world.

Later, when they were leaving the hotel, she had to force a smile when she passed diners she knew. She only hoped it would be good enough.

They drove back almost in total silence, with Mike sound asleep between them. When they stopped out front with the cold night outside the car, Bill reached to straighten his son on the seat because he was leaning on Peggy and said, "I guess I'd better wind things up down here tomorrow and head back for Burlington. I've got an aunt up there who can take him until I can figure something else out."

Peggy looked from the child to his father. "Leave him with me," she said quietly.

They exchanged a long look before Bill shook his head. "Impossible. It's not your headache."

She said, "Headache? *Heart*ache. Bill, let him stay with me. At least for a few days." She laid a warm hand on the man's arm. "Please?"

He did not move for a moment; then he straightened the child, got out, and when he came round to her side of the car, she also got out. The child was sleeping too soundly to realize he was alone.

They walked up to the porch. There, Bill took her by the shoulders. "Look; don't get wrapped up in other people's problems. You can ruin your life doing that."

She looked him squarely in the face. "I can't think of a better way to ruin it."

For five seconds they stood eye to eye, and then he bent gently, kissed her squarely on the mouth, very softly, and pulled back. "You'd better ask your brother. Little kids aren't everyone's cup of tea."

She smiled. "Go get him and bring him into the house where it's warm. I'll tell Earl."

But she couldn't tell Earl because he had already gone to bed.

CHAPTER SEVEN

EARL WAS surprised the following morning, but not because he saw the child; his sister told him over breakfast who was asleep in the downstairs spare bedroom. Earl went to see and returned with a grin.

"He looks about as big as a puppy in that bed."

Over breakfast Peggy explained the dilemma of Michael Harland Tappan and his father. Earl reacted predictably to the story of the woman shipping the little boy to his father the way she had done. He was horrified.

The only place during their discussion she anticipated difficulty was when she told him Mike Tappan would be staying with them for a few days, perhaps a week.

She led up to that so painstakingly that her brother finally put down his coffee cup, looked wryly at her, and said, "Okay; young mister Tappan needs a woman right now, and his father isn't situated to look after him for the time being, and all the rest of what you've been beating around the bush with, Peg. Now tell me: are you going to adopt him or just keep him for Bill Tappan for a while?"

She said, "Keep him for a while. Do you mind terribly, Earl?"

He started to rise from the breakfast table. "I don't mind at all. I think he's a handsome little cuss." He arose and stepped back behind the chair for the jacket hanging on the doorknob. As he donned the jacket, he smiled at her. "He just may be the answer to a hell of a lot of things around here. See you this evening. Oh, by the way, I'll bring the books in tonight."

She did not leave the table until she heard the door close out front; then she rose, cleaned up the kitchen, looked at the thermostat in the parlor to be certain the house was warm enough, and went to get Michael Harland Tappan.

He was already up, very soberly struggling through the complicated process of getting dressed in his white shirt and light blue trousers and jacket. He hadn't touched the tie and he hadn't tied his shoes when she entered. He looked up and without any other greeting said, "I don't tie my shoes very well, you know."

She almost laughed. Instead, she went over, dropped to one knee, and tied the shoes. Then she looked up. Even before he'd washed or combed his mop of light brown hair, he was a handsome little boy. What she really felt, she did not want him ever to know.

They went out to the kitchen. Little boys were always hungry. As for the scrubbing and hair-combing, it could wait. And the clothes were all wrong. He couldn't even go outside in this kind of weather dressed like that.

She made a list of things he'd need: warm, winter clothing, mittens, knitted hat, heavy jacket, everything she could think of. After breakfast she found an old mail order catalog and they lay in front of the fireplace in the living room studying it. He was so engrossed in the color pictures that he did not even glance up when the doorbell rang.

Peggy knew who would be out there. She got up, smoothed her slacks and sweater, looked back, and found that, at least for now, the catalog had replaced her as Michael Harland Tappan's point of focal interest, so she went to open the door.

Bill was there with a bouquet of the reddest roses she had ever seen. The only roses anyone ever found in New England this time of year grew in hothouses, usually down near New York City, and they cost a fortune. She took them, thanked him profusely, and closed the door after him. Their eyes met above the roses. He did not look as though he had slept very well the previous night. Otherwise, though, he was as she always thought of him: broad, lanky, immaculate, even though he seemed most often to dress very casually, more for comfort than for the impression he might make.

She smiled. "On the floor in the living room." Then, as he started to turn, she said, "Bill, did his mother send any clothes with him?"

"No. He came just as you saw him last night."

Peggy's indignation stirred, but only briefly. "Well, he's got to have more than his white shirt and blue jacket. I've made a list. It's in the kitchen. I'll get it."

He reached out as she started past. She turned at his touch, holding the fragrant red roses between them. Whatever reservations she had once had, somewhere along the line between last night and this morning, had quite vanished.

She smiled at him. "Don't say anything. It isn't necessary." She freed herself. "All right?"

He nodded and as she moved away, he turned heavily toward the living room doorway. She looked back as his son made a little squeal, sprang up from in front of the fireplace, and ran to him. Then she went on into the kitchen.

She gave them plenty of time. She wanted to see them together, and yet she did not trust herself to witness their greeting one another, so she found vases for the roses, took her time making the arrangements, and reread her list of the things Mike would need. Finally, she returned to the front of the house, a vase of red roses in each hand.

Bill and his son were on the floor, where she had been with the child, in front of the fireplace. Mike was excitedly showing his father pictures in the catalog. Behind them the fire was cherry red. When Bill raised his head and winked at her, she got a little lump in her throat.

She put one vase of red roses upon the marble-topped table her mother had cherished so much and the other bouquet she put on the hall table in the entry. Then she went back and dropped down on the far side of the child. She handed Bill her list, and the three of them spent a full hour looking for the items in the catalog, making notations about probable sizes, colors, and styles.

Once, when their eyes met above the child's head, she told Bill this was like Christmas. He laughed at her. "Christmas was never this good," he said, and went back to studying the catalog with his son while she studied his profile, the peaceful, long set of his mouth, and the way he managed to keep his shoulder low and close enough so that it touched the child.

Her heart went out to him. If he'd been a perfect stranger, it still would have gone out to him. Intuition told her how awkward and painful life was going to be for a man and a little boy. Everything in life seemed to be organized around a family unit, a child and two parents. Even a child with only a mother could make it, but there did not seem to be any provision in life for a father and a small child alone together.

The way the system worked, men worked for a living and were only home full-time perhaps on weekends. The more she thought about it, the more impossible it became. A child couldn't grow up like a wild animal, free and footloose without roots or ties.

Bill raised his head to speak. She saw the sudden expression of troubled surprise he gave her and realized that her thoughts were showing.

She smiled quickly and grabbed for something to say out of the blue.

"We could go down to the store. I think most of the things shown here are in stock."

He nodded, but then he said, "Listen, Peg. Maybe this isn't such a good idea. I mean—just now you looked tired or something." He started to get up off the floor. When he was fully upright with his back to the fire, he said, "It isn't fair to Earl either. No one has the right to intrude on someone else's life and dump their troubles in their lap."

She stood up facing him, and although she knew exactly how she felt, she didn't know how to explain it. "Earl thinks he's a wonderful little boy."

"Okay, but liking a little boy and having him underfoot are two different things. Peg, I'm a lawyer, I deal in facts and logic."

She had a flash of quick anger. "Bill, I'm a woman, and *I* deal in feelings and emotion. I know; they aren't ever logical. But right now they're better than your logic."

His gaze softened as he considered her. For no real reason she blushed, and that annoyed her so she said, a little belligerently, "Are we going to argue?"

He looked close to laughing down into her face. "Never." He stood a moment in silence, then said, "Remember the day back along the Buckner road? I thought then . . ."

"Never mind what you thought then," she said, hastily.

He sighed. "All right. It was just something I felt, anyway. Something that I probably wouldn't be able to really put into words."

She looked at the child lying on the floor between them. "Try," she said, and this time when she raised her eyes, they both laughed—and she blushed again.

But he didn't try; he teased her instead. "I'll have to think it over; try to find exactly the right words." He reached for one of her hands. "Getting back to that other topic."

She did not pull her hand away, but she said, "If we hurry we can get to the store before Earl goes to lunch. He could probably help us better than Morris could."

He waited a moment. "Peg, I'm not going to do this. It's a terrible imposition. Little kids need constant care and watching. I'll hire a woman here in Brunswick. There's bound to be someone . . ."

"You are going to hire someone?" she asked, and when he nodded, she sprang her trap. "All right. I've just accepted the position. Now let's get down to the store before Earl goes to lunch."

She would have pulled her hand free and reached for the child, but his grip suddenly tightened on her fingers. He pulled slightly. She had to lean. He kissed her as gently as he had that other time. Before he could say anything, she straightened back and finally freed her hand.

"That's not in the contract, *Mr*. Tappan," she said, and knelt down to help Michael Harland

Tappan get up off the floor. Then she glanced up and smiled at him. "But I think I know what it meant."

He had a car outside, a fairly new car. He said he'd rented it for his stay in Brunswick from Jim Burley who owned the garage in town. When they climbed in the car, it was coid so Peggy put part of her jacket around Mike. She would have cuddled him, too, but he seemed to have very definite ideas about when women should do things like that and when they shouldn't; he wriggled free and sat very erectly between them.

Bill threw her a wise look and then drove away in the direction of the business district.

The sky was lighter today than it had been the previous day, and it was possibly a few degrees warmer, but that was not much in the way of mitigation because cold, whether ten below or ten above, was still cold.

Most of the stores had their lights switched on even though it was only a little past noon when they drove down.

The beautiful snow of a couple of days back was now slush; where it had been shoveled off the walks, it lay in dirty piles, and the moving traffic, which was heavier than it had been the last day or two, even though most drivers drove slowly and were considerate, still managed to throw dirty icewater on both sides as the cars cruised along.

Earl was at the store. Morris told them he was in the office working on the books; otherwise, he would have been out to lunch by now. They went back and Peggy knocked. Earl came to open the door. He looked at them with a smile, and then he grinned widest at Mike and bent to extend a large hand. Mike soberly shook, walked inside, and planted himself near the electric heater. He hadn't said anything about being cold, but his trousers and coat and light shirt were certainly not meant for the kind of weather they were having now.

Peggy handed her brother the list. Earl looked from it to Bill Tappan, eyes frankly questioning. Bill answered in an embarrassed way.

"All he has are the clothes he's standing in."

Earl nodded, looked at the list again, then said, "Well, you've come to the right place. Come along, we've got to do some trying-on." As he followed his sister out into the store, he looked around. Mike was not very anxious to leave the heater. Earl went back and held down a hand. "You too, partner."

CHAPTER EIGHT

IT WAS like Christmas. When they left the store, they had no less than nine boxes, and by the time they got back to Peggy's house and inside by the fireplace with their packages, she was almost as breathless with excitement as the child was.

They tried the winter attire on him. She told Bill she had never seen a child look as handsome, and it was the truth. His eyes, large and well-set like the eyes of his father, were alive with appreciation and interest. But she learned something about him here; unlike a lot of children, the more engrossed Mike Tappan was with something, even though he laughed and smiled a lot, the less he said.

They took him out back, where the snow still lay as it had fallen, and watched him fall and roll in it as he struggled to explore the yard. They were side-by-side on the rear porch. To Peggy it was rather like watching a cooped-up puppy after he had been set free, but eventually she thought of something else, something sobering.

"Bill, last night he was dog-tired, and maybe if he keeps playing so hard he'll be that way again tonight. But what do I tell him when I tuck him in one of these nights and he asks me when his mother is coming to see him, or something like that?"

Bill did not look at her; he was still watching his son when he replied. "Don't worry. The only two people who've tucked him in for the past four years, except for a couple of visiting interludes, were my housekeeper back in Burlington and me." He turned and looked at her. "Once, when he was only a couple of years old and his mother came back on one of her money-needing junkets, she tried to put him to bed and he cried; he didn't remember her."

Peggy turned back slowly and watched the child. He had found the old carriage shed, which her father had converted to a large two-car garage and which Earl had made an additional modification to years back, when he'd been in high school, by turning one side of the old building into a sort of machine shop and motor-repair works. Mike tried to climb a snowdrift over there and fell through several times before he walked back; then he turned and studied the drift.

Peggy laughed. "He looks like a little fat elf."

"At times he's more like a little devil," said Bill, and smiled at her. He reached inside his jacket for a small envelope. "I've got to go back to Vermont tomorrow. I'll probably be gone two or three days. This is what I remember about his feeding schedule." She took the envelope as he went on speaking. "I'll be back as quickly as I can."

He paused, and she thought she knew what was coming next, but she waited. "Peg, this isn't at all fair to you. You're too young to be tied down with someone else's kid."

She had her answer to his protest ready and waiting. "Bill, if I didn't want to do this, I'd tell you. As for being tied down—this is exactly what will free me from being tied down. I'm just my brother's housekeeper and bookkeeper." She stuffed the envelope into a pocket. "You stay out here and keep an eye on him while I go inside and start supper. What time is it?"

He looked. "Almost four o'clock. Where did the day go?"

She laughed at his expression. "Where they all go when you're doing something you like to do." She stepped to the door. "If you'd stay and eat with us I'd . . ."

"No," he said, almost fiercely, then checked himself. "Peg, some other time?"

She did not yield. "If I make one of my world-renowned, exotic meatloaves?"

They stood looking at one another, and when she smiled, she knew he'd agree. He said, "But it's a lot of extra bother, and I've already intruded more than I should." His objection sounded more plaintive than insistent.

"When Mike's had his play," she told him, "you can take him to his bedroom. There's a bath adjoining. Scrub him, then dress him, and by then dinner will be ready."

He showed a slow grin. "You sound like a wife."

She went on to the kitchen. There was a lot to do. A lot more than he suspected, but then she knew from having kept house for her brother for so long how little men really understood about a woman's work.

Once, she looked out the back window. Bill was down on his knees in the snow showing his son how to make a snow castle. She shook her head. Bill would be wet and cold; *he* would probably be the one to come down with a cold, not the child.

It had been cold, standing out there in the late day. She made a quick trip to the living room to put more wood on the fire and to check all the rooms, making certain the house would be warm enough; then she returned to the kitchen just in time to see them coming.

She met them at the pantry with an admonition. "No wet shoes beyond this point." She pointed to the corner where she and her brother left their boots. Then she leaned and kissed the child's icy cheek when he stared upward as though she had done or said something that had made him uncertain.

She helped him off with his small laced boots and his soggy jacket. As she removed his cap, she ran a light hand through his hair. "I like you, Michael Harland Tappan."

He leaned impulsively and threw both arms

around her neck and hugged, surprisingly hard for a small child. Then he freed himself and turned to his shoe-less father to be led away.

Peggy stood up with a peculiar little sensation of wonderful pain in her heart.

Then she went back to work, and as she was checking the pre-heated oven before putting the meatloaf in, the telephone rang out in the hall. She popped the pan in, closed the oven, and made a dash for the front of the house.

It was Earl with an excuse and an apology. "Listen, Peg, I was going to bring the books home to you tonight, but somewhere along the way.... Remember that merchandise you brought over from Buckner? Well, Morris and I can't account for some of it."

She was surprised. "But it was all there, Earl, on the dock."

Almost irritably he said, "I don't mean you lost any of it. We checked it in. Morris shelved it, so it was here, but now some of the sales slips don't tally with the invoices and . . ."

She said, "Not stolen, Earl."

"Peg, we've lost some sale slips. That's all. Before I can close the books, that stuff's got to be accounted for. How the hell do we send out the monthly statements and keep our inventory current if we don't have a correct tally? We'll find 'em, but what I called about—I'll get something at the restaurant tonight. Don't wait dinner for me. Okay? See you later."

He rang off.

She put the telephone down slowly. It wasn't

the first time something like this had happened
and it probably wouldn't be the last time,
either. He and Morris would correct the error.
She suddenly thought of something; she hadn't
had the chance to tell him they had company
this evening. She did not call him back; when
he was in the kind of mood he obviously was in
this evening, he wouldn't like being interrupted
by something like dinner guests; that would
only exacerbate the situation for him.

She returned to the kitchen with mixed
feelings. Of the affair at the store she thought
little. Anyone in business knew that these
things happened. It wouldn't be a disaster if the
items were never located. When they took the
next physical inventory the first of next year,
the items would turn up anyway.

What occupied her mind more was the fact
that now she and Bill would be there together.
Little Mike would get sleepy early; it had been
an exciting, rigorous day for him. Afterward. . . .

She looked in at the meatloaf. It was browning
to perfection, but to give it an added touch of
flavor and color, she poured some ketchup over
the top crust, then closed the door and went to
set the table.

The kitchen was warm and fragrant. All her
life she had loved the smell and feel of this
kitchen, of any kitchen in fact, where a woman
ruled whose heart was anchored to that place.
She'd heard people mention the security of the
home, the solid comfort of a fireplace hearth,
but to Peggy Wheaton there had never been a

room in a house that could come close to saying love and care and personal well-being like a kitchen.

She was still setting the table when Bill and Mike came in. The child's face was still rosy, but now it seemed to be the result of scrubbing. His father smiled over at her. "This place smells like heaven," he said. "I haven't eaten since breakfast."

She was horrified. It hadn't occurred to her when he'd arrived about noon that he hadn't eaten. She was disgusted with herself. "Bill, I'm sorry. I just didn't think." She pointed. "Sit down. Put Mike between us. I'll get it on the table right away."

He took his son to the table and laughed. "It doesn't matter. Lots of times I don't eat in the middle of the day."

She got him a cup of coffee, and as she passed Mike's chair she threw him a smile and a wink. He very soberly screwed up one side of his face and winked back. They laughed at him, and a whole host of little nagging things disappeared for Peggy.

She mentioned that Earl had called, while she was over at the sideboard slicing the meatloaf, explained about the lost items, and said he wouldn't be able to get home until later.

Bill wondered the same things she had wondered. "Lost or stolen?" he asked.

"Misplaced, more than likely," she replied, taking their plates to them and then returning for her plate. "It happens every now and then, but Earl's a stickler when it comes to accounting. He and Morris keep a running inventory. I suppose it's all right to do that, but it's always seemed to me to be unnecessary extra work." She looked up, smiling.

"But I wouldn't make a good storekeeper, which is probably why Earl doesn't encourage me working down there."

Bill was already beyond the point of this conversation. He rolled up his eyes in exaggerated ecstasy. "They were right. All those people throughout the world who have written odes to your meatloaf. All those gifted poets and musicians who've bequeathed to mankind the superiority of your Brunswick, Massachusetts, cuisine."

She laughed at him. "The only thing lower on the cooking scale than meatloaf is stew."

"But you've lifted meatloaf to fresh heights," he protested, laughing at her only with his eyes. "You've created a long-overdue counter-culture: a world of people dedicated to love and peace and humility because they've tasted Peg Wheaton's meatloaf."

"You're insane," she said, laughing and blushing at the same time.

Mike ate and concentrated on nothing else. For a child no larger than he was, Michael Harland Tappan could eat more than Peggy had ever seen a child eat. She remembered what old John Bellanger had told her one time when she had picked at food. "A person who don't eat up hearty, Peggy, grows up with a measly body and poorly kind of mind and spirit. You want to grow up all arms and legs and lackadaisicalness?" She hadn't wanted that, of course, so she had started eating, and it wasn't for three years that she found out that "lackadaisicalness" wasn't a wasting disease brought on by being undernourished, but by then she had become a powerful eater, for a child, exactly as Mike was.

Thinking of John Bellanger, she said, "I heard that you bought the Bellanger place."

He nodded between mouthfuls; he, she noted, was also a good eater. "I got three bids the way my client instructed me. Then I telephoned him from the hotel and submitted them. Then I topped the best one by a thousand dollars, and he took it."

She said, "Whatever for, Bill?"

He leaned and gazed at her. "Because I decided a couple of days ago I was going to move to Brunswick."

She saw the look on his face and ignored it. "Brunswick isn't large enough to support a lawyer, is it? I don't remember hearing of anyone suing someone else here in years."

He winked. "Maybe I could get someone's dog to bite a neighbor, then take both sides." He laughed. "My practice isn't lawsuits. Oh, I handle 'em, but my practice is largely estates, water rights, taxes, and so forth. There isn't a town in America that doesn't need a tax lawyer."

She listened, but she was still dubious when she noticed that Mike was slowing down, and that his eyes were getting heavy.

A BROKEN DREAM

The place she had started wildly.....
she...her...lains their

CHAPTER NINE

THERE WOULD come a time in the life of Michael Harland Tappan when getting him to march off to bed would require all the adroitness adults could muster, but tonight was not one of those times. Peggy offered him her hand, and he went with her willingly. The only thing worrying him was the fate of his soggy new boots with the bright yellow lacings, and his father promised solemnly to dry them out and see that they were put beside his bed so that when he arose in the morning they would be there.

Peggy watched him make quite an ordeal of brushing his teeth, and she knelt with him at bedside, half expecting him not to know a prayer. But he knew one; he did not know it very well, but he knew enough of it so she could coach him. Then, when she tucked him in, he looked up at her and said, "I hope you don't go away."

She smiled past the lump in her throat. "Don't worry about that." She kissed him lightly and pulled upright. "If you need me, I'll be close by."

She went out, closed his door two-thirds of the way, and stood in the gloomy hallway waiting for the lump to go away. Perhaps Bill did believe that his son did not know his mother, but Peggy now knew better. She also knew that his son associated his mother with someone who came and went. For a moment, Peggy thoroughly despised that other woman, but only for a moment; she wasn't a judge and hadn't been put here to be one.

She went to the parlor, which was empty, and then went back to the kitchen. Bill was humming to himself, sleeves rolled up at the sink. She would have taken over but he held up a dripping hand. "You dry them and put them away." He winked at her. "This is the warmest my hands have been all day."

She told him what his son had said, and for a while he worked in silence, and even when he eventually commented, he did it slowly.

"When I was in college I had a few courses in psychology. I didn't get much from it that I hadn't halfway figured out for myself just from being around people. But there was one thing that's stuck in my head ever since. People are largely formed in childhood. Broken homes ruin more kids than anything else does. I tried like hell to cope with that; I didn't want Mike growing up as some kind of misfit, some kind of insecure individual who had all kinds of dark twists and hangups.

"But the hell of it is, there's something the

psychology books I read neglected to tell you and that is simply that in some cases keeping a kid's mother around so he'll feel wanted and loved and secure can wreck him in other ways. He can learn, for example, how to promise things, then never do them, how to tell simple little lies that eventually became damned big lies. So—I told her the last time she left that if she ever did it again, never to come back." He looked up. "She won't."

Peggy wondered. "How can you be so sure she won't."

He smiled without humor. "Because she cleaned out my bank accounts this time." At Peggy's stare, he shrugged and went back to the dishes.

"She did it by forgery, but she knew I wouldn't prosecute, and she was right. It's almost worth it just to be able to draw a fresh, clean breath and feel the whole damned load sliding off my shoulders. Now, all I have to do is cut loose from all the rest of it; from her drinking friends, the creditors who used to show up at my office every month or two, the whole damned lot."

He finished the last dish, pulled the drain-plug, and accepted the clean hand-towel Peggy offered him.

"And you wondered why anyone would want to practice law in a place like Brunswick. I'll tell you exactly why, Peg. Even if Mike and I starve, at least we'll have snow and mountains and Miller's pond . . . and other wonderful things around here ... to enjoy while we're starving. Anyway, we don't need the kind of money I made up in Vermont to live down here.

"And there are some bonds my wife couldn't get her hands on. We'll make it for three or four years if I don't find a single client." He handed back the towel and looked over at her. "Now I've dumped *that* on your shoulders as well. You must think I'm an awful mess."

She turned to take the plates to the cupboard, and as she put them away, her back to him, she said, "She'll still be your wife, Bill."

He examined his puffy, pink hands. "Only until I can get the divorce rammed through. I'll start that in Burlington tomorrow. I'll also start liquidating up there." She turned, and as their eyes met across the room, he said, "Peg—oh, nothing. You've got about all one human needs for now."

They went out to the living room where the fire was smouldering down to cherry embers. There were only two lights burning, the one in the entry-hall, which she always left on when her brother came home late, and the end-table lamp by the couch that half-faced the fireplace. He sank down next to that lamp, pushed out his long legs, and smiled up at her. "Did you ever have a premonition that you were coming home?"

She sat down beside him. She'd never had that particular premonition, but she'd had others, and right now she did not want to talk about the one that was in her mind.

She sought to keep what had to become a personal conversation from becoming one by saying, "Maybe, if you handle all those other things, like estates and taxes, you could make a living around here, Bill." She had an idea. "Talk to Earl. He's knowledgeable about things like that."

He lay an arm across the back of the sofa behind her and leaned back, completely relaxed. "I already have," he replied. "Earl and I didn't just discuss your meatloaf and my client's inheritance." She looked around, but he was gazing half-drowsily up at the ceiling as he spoke.

"That's what I was going to tell you yesterday; well, at least there's a kind of connection. I talked to your brother the day after we met. We talked for over an hour. He thought a lawyer could make it around Brunswick. He said it might take a year or two to get well-established, but he said he was sure in that length of time I could make it." He slowly dropped his eyes and turned his head to her. "The connection is simply that when I first met you there at the side of the road, and we stood talking, I could feel the affinity. What could you call it, I wonder? It was a sort of peace in me that came from you." He slowly smiled. "Sounds pretty crazy, doesn't it? Maybe a century from now that's how people will . . ."

"Would you like some coffee?" she asked,

leaning to arise. His arm touched her shoulder gently, holding her in place without effort.

"Peg . . . ?"

She couldn't make herself move, but she did not face him. "Yes?"

"I guess I just did it all wrong at the outset, didn't I?"

She had all but forgotten. She leaned back again, still with his arm on her shoulder. She did not reply right away; she did not know *how* to reply. She didn't want this to get personal, but of course it had to and she knew that too, but the moment she answered him—if she answered truthfully—it was certainly going to get even more personal.

He twisted a little, slowly, and turned her face gently toward him with his free hand. "Everything happens at once, doesn't it?" he said. "One day you're driving back from Buckner, and the next day someone comes along and fouls up your entire life—and is still fouling it up."

She reached up and took his hand away from her chin. She held it in her lap. "Don't talk like that. I'm thankful you both came along. I really am."

She knew what was going to happen and yielded herself up to it without having to make any wrenching adjustments; it was really very easy. She lay her head sideways upon the back of the couch, and when his lips came close, she closed both eyes, raised her arms to his shoulders, and let every emotion respond to his intimate touch.

It was so fundamental, so basically simple and honest, the way that she responded to him, that long afterward she wondered how she had ever been able to believe she shouldn't respond to him like that.

She loved him, and that was simple and honest, too. She had no idea when it had suddenly resolved itself in her head or heart, but it had. She knew it the moment he touched her, there on the couch. She loved him with all the pent-up lifelong hunger of a girl who had matured late but who was a full woman now. She had a depth of passion she had never suspected, and although it left her feeling drained empty afterward, at the moment she clung to his lips and gave back every soft-fierce demand he made of her.

Then someone stamping up onto the front porch made her heart nearly stop. Everything turned to ash and she fought clear. Earl was scuffing off his overshoes outside. Peggy rose none too steadily and went over by the fireplace where she turned and looked back with eyes as large and as sultry-dark as new agate.

Bill spoke so softly the words did not carry beyond her. "I love you; I started loving you that day beside the Buckner road."

Earl opened the door, came inside, paused in the entry-hall to shed his jacket and hat, and then came into the living room entrance. At sight of Bill he smiled in surprise.

"She fed you meatloaf," he said. "I can detect

the fragrance. You know, that's how that Greek
goddess tried to kill all those sailors that tied
each other to the mast or something. It wasn't
really her music that made them her slaves, it
was her meatloaf."

Bill laughed and got up to shake Earl's hand.
Peggy watched them like that and decided that
they were alike in many ways; more than just
being alike, they complemented one another.

She said, "Earl, did you eat dinner?"

He nodded at her almost casually. "An hour
and a half ago. But it wasn't meatloaf; it
was—believe it or not—oyster stew." He shrugged
his shoulders as though to indicate he'd had no
alternative. Then he beamed at her.

"And we found the missing merchandise. I
was sure Morris had forgotten to write up those
items. I guess secretly he was sure I had because
when we finally found the stuff, it was off my
shelves in the hardware department, and Morris
was so pleased he stood in front of the counter
grinning from ear to ear."

Earl laughed and Bill smiled, but Peggy
simply stood over there gazing dispassionately
at her brother. For a moment or two Earl did
not feel anything. He was a simply, direct man
with few sensitive tendrils; when he entered a
room he accepted everything at face value, but
even that kind of basically honest and uncom-
plicated individual did not possess the hide of
an elephant. Eventually, Earl began to sense
something.

He finally said, "Well, I thought I'd have a

nightcap, then go to bed. Could I interest either one of you?"

Bill declined and Peggy shook her head, still gazing at him almost impassively. He looked back at her and seemed, finally, to get a dawning little suspicion. He grinned at them. "Well, in that case . . ."

He turned, but halfway through the door, he turned back, remembering something. "Goodnight, Bill. Drop by for coffee again when you can." His sobering glance lingered upon his sister. "See you in the morning." He went on out of the room.

Peggy waited until she heard the kitchen door close, and then she looked at Bill and said, "I think I'm glad he came along when he did." But when he stood waiting, mute and patient, she left her position in front of the fireplace and went over into his arms. It was like flint on steel; like lightning striking a forest; like a man touching a woman who had been waiting so long for that to happen.

She said, "Tell me again."

He told her again, and he proved it in the best of all ways that two people could prove their love for one another. She never did tell *him,* not that night anyway. She didn't have to tell him; she *showed* him.

Afterward, she was exhausted and limp, and being close beside him with her eyes closed, she felt instinctively that no matter what happened, no matter how long she lived, she would never

again feel as she felt now. This only happened
once; it was what life was all about. And as she
struggled against sleep, she was willing to cry
or laugh or just lie close to him like that,
whatever he wanted of her.

CHAPTER TEN

HE CALLED her the next morning, late, to promise he'd be back as soon as he could tear free in Burlington.

The sun was out this morning, the sky had miraculously cleared. She accepted this, and the autumnal warmth, as part of some ritual that had to follow their declaration of love. She didn't even hear the telephone when Harriett called, not just because she'd finished bundling Mike up before turning him loose out back, but because her mind wasn't functioning rationally yet. But eventually she heard it and went through the house believing it would be Earl, but it wasn't.

The first thing Harriett said was, "Hey, you three looked like a staid middle-class family out for their weekly dinner, like all the rest of Brunswick's solid burghers, the other night. Is that really *his* little boy? He's so adorable, Peg. Even my dad, who doesn't ever say much about children, thought he was handsome—not *him*— the child. And you looked so—I don't know what it was—so sort of statuesque and *satisfied*."

Peggy leaned on the wall waiting for the tirade to run down so she could get a word in. But Harriett had stout lungs.

"Of course, you know he bought the Bellanger place. My dad said he thinks he's going to move here and open up a law office. Dad thinks we need a lawyer in Brunswick. But that little boy!"

Peggy finally said, "Harriett!"

The answer came back after a pause. ". . . Yes?"

"Do you really want answers, or do you just want to ask the questions and also answer them?"

Harriett sighed. "Do you know what I *really* want?"

Peggy's heart softened. "Please don't tell me," she said quietly.

"By any chance, has he a brother, Peg?"

"Not that I know of." It struck Peggy that she really knew next to nothing about Bill; that is, she knew next to nothing about him *personally*. About his family and his growing-up period, his éducation, and all that.

"But the little boy *is* his, isn't he?" asked Harriett.

"Yes."

"Then he's married," exclaimed Harriett.

Peggy was baffled by that, too. "Well, yes, he's married. And in case you haven't had your ear to the ground today, he's gone back to Vermont for a few days."

Harriett's voice echoed with curiosity when she said, "He has, really?"

Peggy almost smiled. "For two or three days; then he'll be back. And it's true that he bought John Bellanger's house and plans to open a law office here."

Harriett listened, but clearly these were not things that actually interested her except insofar as they were relevant to Bill Tappan as an individual. She said, "He sure confides in you a lot, Peg," and for a moment Peggy had to bite her tongue before trusting herself to speak.

In a level tone she said, "What's new down at the drug store?"

But Harriett Stokes could presume on a friendship reaching back to childhood, so she answered that with a question that ignored even the existence of her father's drug store.

"Did he take his little boy back with him?"

This time Peggy had a harder struggle of it, holding back her resentment. "Harriett, for heaven's sake!"

At once the curious, hazel-eyed girl retreated. She probably recognized the danger sounds in her friend's voice. "I'm sorry," she said, speaking fast. "I know what I'm doing. I mean, I know I'm acting like Mrs. Burley or some of the other town gossips. Peg, I think I'll go over to Boston."

It was such an abrupt switch that Peggy was left high and dry. "Boston? Whatever for?"

"Oh, I don't know. Yes, I do. I don't want to dry up and wither away here in Brunswick, and that's sure as hell what's going to happen to me if I don't break out of here. Over there I can get a job, have my own apartment, meet people. . . . You understand, don't you?"

Peggy understood, exactly. "Yes. Care to come over this afternoon and cry on my shoulder?"

Harriett's moment of dissatisfaction seemed to pass in a twinkling. "I'd love to. As soon as I finish the housework."

Peggy said, quite dryly, "Be prepared for a shock. I've got Michael Harland Tappan."

". . . You've got who?"

"Bill Tappan's little boy. I'm keeping him for Bill."

". . . You *are*?" Peggy put down the telephone, groaned to herself, and went out to the kitchen where she could see into the back garden. Michael Harland Tappan was working very diligently adding rooms that resembled reject doughnuts to the snow-castle his father had started for him the day before. She watched for a long time. The child had an almost aggressive purpose and drive to his actions. He seemed unaware of everything else in the world but that snow-castle.

She went, eventually, to do her housework, and she went through the entire routine without once telling her hands what to do. Habit was a wonderful thing; it was also a terrible thing. It depended upon the goal and aspirations of the person with the habit.

Finally, she went back to get Mike and bring him in for some hot beef broth. He talked more than he ever had before, all about his snow-castle.

His entire face lighted up when he talked. Even when she took him to his room to change into dry clothes and he climbed up onto the bed as though it were a duty, he was still so engrossed in his work outside in the snow that for a few moments she did not understand why he had climbed onto the bed. Because he thought he was supposed to take a nap, of course.

She drew a cover over him, then sat on the edge of the bed until the warmth began to change his mood. When his eyes closed, finally, she kissed him and tiptoed out into the hallway.

She was learning. Up until now, everything she had done had been motivated by female instinct. She decided that wasn't going to be enough. There would be books at the library.

She went out back where he had left his boots, and as she bent to retrieve them so she could put them where they would dry, she saw the tip of an envelope jutting from one of the pockets of her jacket and remembered the letter Bill had given her. She took it back to the kitchen with her, left it upon the table until she had set Mike's boots to dry, then went over and sat down to read whatever he had written.

As Bill had said, the envelope held a series of enumerated things such as which foods his son liked best, when he took his nap—which she had just found out by herself—and several other things. But the folded green slip of paper that had been slid into the envelope, along with those other little tips on child care, stopped her cold. It was a check for one hundred and fifty dollars, and at the bottom of the note Bill had written. "If it isn't enough, tell me when I get back and we'll make an adjustment. This is for the first week's care."

She sat gazing at the check. Not only was it far too much, but she didn't even like to think of taking money from him, particularly not for caring for Mike.

And yet it had been *she*, when he had mentioned hiring someone local to look after his son, who had said she would take the job. Under those circumstances she could hardly feel indignant.

It wasn't exactly indignation that she felt anyway; it was more like disappointment or chagrin or something along those lines. She didn't know exactly what she felt, but there was something—terrible—about taking money from a man the morning after . . .

She arose, took the note, the envelope, and the check to her room, put them out of sight in a dressing-table drawer, and looked at herself in the mirror. She looked pale, so she went to scrub her face in cold water. That restored the color, but the look in her eyes did not change.

Harriett wouldn't notice. Harriett had never been very observant; her effervescent kind of person seldom was. They exploded into the world each morning like the newly-risen summer sunshine, blinding everything around them with energy and activity.

Poor Harriett. She was right; there was nothing in Brunswick for someone like her, and right up until last night—well, maybe a day or two before last night—there really hadn't been anything in Brunswick for Peggy either. She had sensed it in her increasing restlessness lately.

But this morning she was in a changed world.

She went back to the kitchen, made a fresh pot of coffee, steeled herself for Harriett's visit, and went to the living room to see if there was any chance of poking fresh life into the fire from last night. There wasn't, but the sun was shining and the house was warm anyway.

She went to her room and changed into slacks and a thick, loose sweater—and looked at herself again in the mirror. She looked normal now.

The doorbell rang. She went to answer almost with dragging footsteps. But it wasn't Harriett; it was Frank Beasley, the elfin bus depot stationmaster. Brunswick did not have a railroad spur, so the only public transportation that passed through town was the bus.

Frank was grinning from ear to ear as he handed her a large, long, pale green box. "Flowers," he announced with pride and delight as though he had brought them to her as a personal present. "You know, Peggy, it costs a sight of money to buy flowers this time of year and ship 'em by bus."

She smiled as he handed over the box. "Thank you, Frank."

He bobbed his head up and down like a bird but only shuffled his feet instead of turning away to depart. "They wouldn't be from Earl.

Maybe from that young buck who minds the
station over at Buckner."

She kept smiling. "Maybe. Thank you very
much for delivering them, Frank."

He finally had to concede defeat, but he did it
gracefully. "My pleasure, Peggy. Surely my
pleasure. Been a long time in Brunswick since
any of the ladies got flowers sent to 'em like
that."

She closed the door, went to the kitchen,
opened the box, and found a dozen long-stemmed
red roses with a little note. She read the note,
blushed, re-read it, and then went to find vases
for the roses.

It was criminal to waste money like this. He
didn't have to send roses; she would have felt
just as—whatever it was she now felt: love,
heartache, pride, longing, humility—if he'd just
sent her the note with the same brief, very
personal message on it.

She didn't even think how Harriett would
react until she had the vases set out in the
parlor, and she was admiring the roses when
the doorbell rang again. But *then* she thought
of that; for a terrible moment she almost panicked, almost grabbed the vases and fled to the
kitchen with them. But of course that's where
she and Harriett would go to sit and have their
coffee. So in the end she simply went out to
open the door and face whatever ensued.

There was no way to explain away twelve
long-stemmed roses to someone as love-starved
as Harriett Stokes, and Peggy did not intend

even to try and tell a little lie because Harriett knew when Peggy's birthday was as well as Peggy knew herself.

She opened the door and Harriett came in, wearing that little fur cap again, and when she turned to shed her coat she looked through the hallway into the parlor and saw the roses. She stopped moving until the shock had passed; then she finished hanging up her coat and turned to Peggy with her hazel eyes as large as marbles.

"Wow!" she said. "Red roses this time of year?"

The hazel eyes clung to Peggy like leeches. There was a way to at least postpone the explanation, so Peggy said, "The coffee's perking. Come along to the kitchen."

CHAPTER ELEVEN

IT WASN'T until that night when she was lying in bed that the funny part of it hit Peggy, and she smiled in the darkness.

Poor Harriett, she had wanted so much to delve right down to the bottom of whatever was going on between Bill Tappan and Peggy Wheaton, but she had been frustrated by the kind of tact that kind of probing demanded. Nor had Peggy helped very much; all she'd ever admitted was what Harriett already knew: that she had gone to dinner with Bill and that she was keeping his child for him until he returned from Vermont. Everything else Peggy had turned aside easily and unrelentingly, until she *had* finally admitted that the roses had come from Bill. But even that hadn't come out until they had drunk three cups of coffee and had moved on to the living room.

Then the humorous part of it had ended, and Harriett had poured out her personal frustrations; there were eligible men in town who came around, and some married men who had hinted

they would like to come around. When Harriett
had spoken of the latter, her hazel eyes had
shown disgust. When she'd mentioned the former,
she'd looked up at Peggy with an expression of
candid exasperation. She didn't want to marry
some farmer and have a child every year and
get fat and dowdy.

So Boston, or some large city, seemed to be
her only salvation. Peggy hadn't argued against
leaving Brunswick. She'd never liked the role
of adviser, and she'd never especially liked
being someone's confidant either, but among
girls, and now women too, evidently, that seemed
inevitable. Maybe she looked like a father-con-
fessor—a mother-confessor? She turned onto
her side, closed her eyes, saw Bill's smile in her
mind, and went to sleep with a sigh.

The following morning she fed her menfolk,
and Earl got little Mike to laughing at the
breakfast table, then went cheerily off to the
store—leaving Peggy with a little boy on her
hands who had hiccups. They didn't leave until
after ten o'clock, when the child was out working
on his melting snow-castle.

Peggy had just put Mike down for his nap
after lunch when Bill called from Burlington.
Her heart nearly stopped, then sped up when
she heard his voice.

She told him how lovely the red roses were.
She also made a weak remonstrance about
spending that kind of money. He laughed at
her.

"How else can a man who's not there say I love you?"

She said, "A note . . . ?"

He rejected that. "It has to be something you can feel against your cheek, something you can hold in your hand and admire. It has to project the beauty of a sentiment."

She was surprised. "You're poetic, Bill."

He cleared his throat. "Well, as a matter of fact I read that on an ad in the florist's shop over in Buckner."

She laughed. "When will you be back?"

"That's what I called to tell you. It'll probably be a day longer than I expected. I've got some legal work here I've got to get rid of first."

She hid her disappointment. "Next Friday then?"

He thought so. "Yes, but if something comes up between now and then I'll call you. How's Mike?"

"Fine. He had the hiccups, but they passed. The snow is melting fast now and he's having a hard time keeping the snow-castle from dissolving."

He paused a moment, then said, "Will you marry me, Peg?"

It was one of those sudden switches in a conversation that invariably left her hanging. She had never been able to make that kind of practically instantaneous adjustment to things she hadn't been thinking about, and hadn't been anticipating, that some people could make.

"Well, yes," she said, after a moment, "but you're not free yet. How long does that take, Bill?"

"A lot longer in New England than it takes out in Reno," he replied. "We're behind the times up here in some things. But we'll work that out when I get back. Peg . . . I think about you every evening, and all through the days as well."

She smiled. "That's odd. I thought I was the only one with that affliction."

"Do you love me?"

"Yes. Do you doubt it?"

"You've never told me, Peg."

She blushed and was thankful there was no one to see it. "All right. I love you, Bill. I love you very, very much."

The blushing embarrassment spread all over. "We'd better ring off now; this is costing money. Goodbye, sweetheart."

"All my heart, Peg."

She put down the telephone. It never once crossed her mind that Brunswick's telephone exchange was one of those manually-operated ones, even though she'd known this all her life and knew for a fact that most of the secret gossip around town—which never managed to remain secret for very long—originated among the women who ran the telephone exchange. Right then she didn't have room in her mind for anything other than the soft-said, intimate words that still echoed in her thoughts.

Even afterward, when she went to get Mike

up and dressed, she did not think of this. But she *did* think of something else; she'd forgotten to mention that check, and she'd fully intended to bring that up and scold him a little about it the next time they talked.

A lot of things kept her too busy to remember the source of local gossip. When her brother came home that evening, he had a large cardboard box under one arm, but he said nothing about this until after they had all eaten supper. Then he winked and took Mike into the living room with him. When she went in later, Mike and Earl were busily assembling an electric train set on the floor. Earl had pushed back the rugs because, he said, the jointed track had to rest on something hard.

Mike looked up at her and smiled just once, a sort of dutiful tribute, then he went to work with Earl, and although they spoke now and then together, this was obviously a world that had no place for women in it. She watched them for a while, marveling that anyone Earl's age could make such an easy transition back to age four. It dawned on her for the first time that Earl would have made a wonderful father. Suddenly, she felt terribly sorry for her brother; it had never occurred to her before that if he hadn't had to finish raising her, hadn't had to jump into the general store business when by rights, *natural* rights anyway, he should have been out seeking a wife and starting a family, by now Earl probably would have his own family.

They finished putting the track together, set the engine upon it, hooked on the cars, and when Earl plugged in the transformer, he warned Mike to swing the activating lever slowly, at first, until they could be certain everything was arranged properly. Peggy sat on the edge of her chair as engrossed as they were. Mike pressed his lips together, and when Earl nodded, the child moved the lever very gently, his eyes glued to the engine. It began to move, very slowly, pulling the brightly-colored cars along the track. At a certain place, where the engine crossed some kind of small metal device fitted to the track, it made a high, moaning wail, and Mike's mouth dropped open in surprise. Earl laughed, Mike laughed with him, and Peggy smiled at them both.

She neglected to tell Earl about Bill's telephone call. It wouldn't have really interested him anyway. When she finally remembered and could have told him, he and Mike had decided upon some major changes in the course of the track; instead of having a long, narrow oval, they had decided to re-route the track and create a figure-eight. By then, mentioning the telephone call, or anything else short of the end of the world, for that matter, wouldn't have earned from either of them more than a blank stare.

She went, eventually, to take a hot bath, not minding in the least being temporarily left out of Mike's world. It was bound to happen. She lay in the hot water thinking that as time passed, it was bound to happen more and more; first with the train, then with a tricycle, with kites and baseballs and only the Lord knew what—eventually cars and girls.

That jolted her; not because she'd been thinking in terms of Mike and girls but because she'd allowed her mind to wander over the years, had allowed it to make her much older as it had carried Mike along almost to the threshold of maturity.

And all that time she would be his mother.

The idea of being a mother wasn't altogether novel; she'd accepted that years ago as her destiny and duty, but having it arrive like a ton of lead while she was relaxing in a tub of hot water, while she was still young and unmarried, and while her lover's son was still a small child, had been both insidious and jarring.

She closed her eyes and dwelled upon many different aspects of her current situation. She also thought of other children, hers and Bill's children. She was still floating both in mind and body when Earl came to the outer door and called to her.

"Hey, Harriett Stokes is on the phone. Shall I tell her you'll call back?"

Peggy came back to reality with a slight sensation of annoyance. "Yes. Tell her I'm in the tub and will call her in the morning."

That broke the entire sequence of her ecstatic thoughts, for which she did not thank either of them, her brother or her girlfriend, but it was time to get Mike to bed anyway. So she left the tub, toweled off, put on her nightgown, belted the satin, quilted robe her brother had given her last Christmas, and went to the bedroom for slippers and to sit a moment brushing her hair.

Her face, in the mirror, looked more full, more mature. The sensuous mouth lay soft without pressure and the full, round chin and jaw seemed more relaxed, more mature.

She smiled at herself. Nothing, not even *that*, could have worked such an instantaneous change in her. Human chemistry *did* respond to alterations in the human mind, obviously, but not this quickly. And yet the very dark blue eyes were different, everything in her expression seemed different, so perhaps what she'd believed earlier had been wrong, perhaps the abrupt change in feeling did actually create a different physical aspect.

She didn't dwell on it. She didn't really care. What mattered was that she would be waiting until Friday arrived.

She went to the living room and told Earl it was time for Mike to go to bed. They both looked up as though she had materialized in the form of a hydra-headed dragon—dragoness. She almost laughed at the expressions they turned to her, but instinct told her, for Mike's sake at any rate, she should not smile as though she might relent.

Earl sighed and sat up. He and Mike exchanged a look, and Earl shrugged as though to imply that there was no appeal against this kind of injustice. Little Mike arose very slowly, keeping

one small hand upon the lever of the transformer
until the very last moment.

Earl said, "Well, I'll tell you how we can get
around this, son. Get up an hour early in the
morning."

Mike accepted this suggestion like a drowning
man grabbing at a log. He smiled at Earl, and
when Peggy reached for his fingers, he kept
looking back at her brother. He had just found
not only a good friend but an ally.

She took him to bed, helped him say his
prayers, and when she tucked him in he said,
"Is he my uncle?"

Peggy leaned, kissed him, and pulled back,
nodding. "He's your uncle, sweetheart."

"Are you my aunt?"

It would have been very easy to say yes to
that also, but later on there could be traumatic
repercussions. Men did not marry their own
sisters, and whether Mike understood this now
or not, he certainly would understand it later.
What wasn't going to be an easy thing for him
ever to understand—the mystery of his real
mother—would only be further complicated.

She smoothed back his tumbled hair. "Your
father will be home Friday. I'll let him answer
that. Okay?"

He agreed. "Okay. Shall I kiss you goodnight?"

She leaned, got wetly kissed, stood up, and
said, "Are you going to dream about trains
tonight?"

They smiled at each other; then she doused
the light and went soundlessly out of the room.

In the hall, before going on to the living room where she could hear the little train running, she decided that she hadn't better put off going to the town library and getting some of those books on raising children. Then she walked to the parlor and found Earl making still another change in the arrangement of the train tracks.

CHAPTER TWELVE

SHE GOT the books at the library the following morning, stopped at the Varnum place with Mike and had lunch with Harriett, then went over to the store to pick up a few items needed at home. She introduced Mike to Morris Jackson, her brother's graying, widower clerk. Morris matched Mike's solemnity as they shook hands. Then he looked at Peggy and said, "Now I understand why Earl took so much time selecting exactly the right electric train."

Her brother had gone across to the restaurant for lunch, so she and Morris and Mike, collaborated on getting the items she'd made a list of, and afterward she and Mike headed back home.

He did not ask endless questions like most small children did, although he was curious about everything and interested; he seemed to want to know only about specific things. She hadn't yet figured out his pattern of thought, but she would in time, she thought.

He had another characteristic she admired but also wondered a little about: he could play entirely by himself for hours. He did not seem to need another child to use as a foil or as a sounding board.

But there were certainly advantages to that. She was able to keep up with her housework very easily, and she also had time to read the books on child-rearing and child psychology she'd brought back from the library.

By Friday morning, when Bill was due back, she had read enough on the theory of raising small children to feel quite confident. She also had read enough on that topic to be suspicious of the people who wrote the books she'd brought home. They dealt, perhaps out of necessity, in a wide latitude of generalities; only rarely did they plot a definite sequence of behavior patterns. She began to suspect that they really didn't know how to define something as variable and illusive as childhood behavior and psychology and instead of coming right out and admitting it, had written books that did not really inform a reader as much as they attempted to pin down and define the writer's own thoughts on the subject.

She decided that, in her own position, what was going to be required was an entirely open mind and an ability to field pitches that she had no idea were coming, like that one about her being Mike's aunt.

She had never actually been notable as a swift, spontaneous thinker, but she had no illusions about having to become one now or end up looking like a dolt in little Mike's eyes.

She would never allow that to happen, so she went to meet him each time from then on, balancing forward on her mental toes, and, miraculously, she actually came up with what she thought was a fairly good answer when Mike heard a car drive up out front and left the train long enough to look out the window. As he turned to announce that it was his father, she said, "Let's feed him some lunch before we ask him a lot of questions, shall we?" and Mike smiled conspiratorially at her.

It was her first step into the psychology of childhood, and it worked. When Bill came to the door and she admitted him, he kissed her, then opened his arms for his son. When Mike hurled himself forward, the child said, "You can play with my train right after we've fed you."

Peggy laughed. Mike took his father to see the train, and Peggy had to be very patient because Mike had all that meticulous explaining to do. It dawned on her very gradually that the child had absorbed an enormous amount of actually quite technical information. He must have picked it up from Earl, but she doubted that Earl had explained those things with any actual hope that a four-year-old would either understand them or remember them. As she stood listening, her impatience dwindled and she gazed at the child with fresh appreciation— and a little uneasiness.

They left Mike in the parlor with the train and went to the kitchen. As soon as they had the door closed behind them, Bill reached for her, lay both hands upon her waist, and swayed her into him. She went very willingly. She clung to his mouth with both arms raised round his shoulders. It seemed so completely natural to yield to him; when she was like this she could conceive of nothing that ever had to change for her throughout the duration of her life. Everything was as it had been ordained to be. Then the telephone rang, and as she came back down slowly to the other world, the one of people and telephones, she had to lean against him for a moment until the strength to move returned.

He smiled and went out to the entry-hall with her. As she answered the telephone—half-expecting the caller to be her brother because he was the only person who had ever interrupted their love-making before—Bill ambled on through to the living room and dropped to one knee near his son. The electric train scurried on its noisy way as Peggy said, "Good morning," into the telephone.

The voice that came back was familiar. It belonged to a woman named Edith Gordon, a widow whose husband had left her several business buildings on Main Street, which supplied her with a comfortable living from rents. She had never been a woman Peggy had liked, but since there had been very little to draw them together, Peggy had never really felt anything stronger than disapproval.

Edith Gordon said, "Good morning, child. I just called to ask if there's anything I can do to help you raise that poor, unfortunate little boy."

Peggy hung there, gradually feeling cold all over. Edith Gordon was one of Brunswick's most notorious gossips. Peggy did not have to know any more to guess what was in Edith Gordon's mind.

In a level tone of voice, Peggy said, "No thank you. But it's kind of you to offer, Mrs. Gordon."

"Well," stated the older woman, speaking flatly, a little harshly, "you know of course that with his kind of background, child, he'll need a lot of extra care. Psychiatry, in fact, I should imagine, later on."

Peggy's cold anger began to stir. "Why would he ever need anything like that, Mrs. Gordon?"

The older woman made a little sniffing sound. "Now, Peggy, you can't hide the truth from him forever, you know."

"No one is ever going to hide the truth from him," Peggy retorted, holding her voice down with an effort. "Why should they?"

"Illegitimacy is something people just never quite learn to accept and live with."

Peggy formed the word with her lips but did not say it aloud. She looked past the living room entrance where Bill and the child were busy with the electric train. She suddenly wished that Bill would come to her, hold her, right that minute. She felt an urgent need for him.

But then, almost instantly, she speculated on what effect a revelation to Bill would have. He might react with disillusionment and disgust, might even pack up and leave. And she could not bear the thought of that. Bill, now, was the one man, the only man who mattered to her.

Finally, she said, "Mrs. Gordon, where did you hear that?" and at once the older woman turned wary.

"Margaret, these things will out. That's what I meant about hiding things from the child; it simply can't be done indefinitely. You deserve help. You also should be warned in advance. I've read of cases where that kind of child grew into the most ungrateful and fearful kind of man. There is a counseling service up in Morristown; I'd advise you to contact them before the problem gets beyond you. . . . And of course there would be your association with the child's father . . . Think about it, child, and remember, as a friend of your dead mother, I'm always here if you need me. Goodbye."

Peggy put down the telephone with a cold but steady hand. Fortunately, Bill and Mike were too engrossed with the electric train to look up. She was as white as snow. Without looking into the parlor again, she went along to her bedroom, sat down near the window, and slowly let it all come back until the coldness left and a slow-rising, fierce anger began to replace it.

Bill would be furious. As a lawyer, he would know exactly what to do; first, there would be Edith Gordon, then there would be . . . Peggy suddenly reddened; she knew, finally, where it had started, and what made her wince was the recollection of the things she and Bill had said over the telephone to one another—while one of the local switchboard operators had been deliberately, and avidly, listening in.

She could have cried; except for her anger she might have. It took a few minutes for her normal calmness to return.

She decided, finally, to say nothing to Bill for the time being, and with that decision made, she went to wash her face, brush her hair, and eventually return to the parlor where her lover and his son were still on the floor.

If Edith Gordon had heard some sick mind's distortion of the facts about little Mike, what had she heard about Peggy and Bill Tappan? Peggy couldn't face that and went to the window to look out, where a cold, high wind was whipping and twisting tree limbs. The raw, stark wonder of winter suddenly became a harsh, bitter interlude of vicious spitefulness.

Bill came over behind her, placed his hands upon her shoulders, and turned her gently. She had to force her lips upward at their outward corners, had to compel the anguish to yield to a small smile with her eyes as he said, "I've got to go down to the Bellanger place and make some plans for the boxes and crates that'll start arriving in a day or two." He kissed her cold cheek. "I know Mike doesn't want to come; he's got his train. How about you?"

She didn't think she could stand the drive through town. "Someone has to stay with Mike," she told him.

Bill nodded as though he had already guessed some such answer would come from her. "Okay. But tomorrow we're going to find someone who can sit with him, and then we're going for a long drive through the hills. I've been thinking of that for a week. Just you and me, in the countryside. All right?"

She leaned against him, closed her eyes tightly, and worked her head up and down. "All right."

She went out to the car with him—it was his own car this time; whatever had been wrong with it before must have been repaired at Burley's garage—and watched him drive off. Then she returned to the house, sat a while watching Mike play with the train, and thought of telephoning Earl. But she shrank from going near that telephone.

She remembered that she'd forgotten all about feeding Bill again and shook her head. Where had all that beauty and contentment gone that she'd known only a few minutes ago in his arms in the kitchen?

Mike finally came over and leaned against her knees. He was hungry. She fed him, sat with him, and when they talked at the kitchen table, the child was able to do for her what she hadn't been able to do for herself: bring her back to some kind of reasoning perspective.

What it really amounted to was that Edith Gordon, and perhaps another half-dozen women like her in town, had learned enough from an eavesdropping telephone operator to work up

their own distorted version, not only of little
Mike's appearance in Brunswick with only a
father but of Peggy's association with that man.

How far would it spread? Only as far as
people would listen to it without reacting in
anger. Generally, although there was always
some kind of gossip going around in Brunswick,
in every small town on the face of the earth
such viciousness eventually went beyond what
most people would tolerate. It militated against
the average person's natural liking of other
people, particularly people such as the Wheatons,
whom most of them had known all their lives.

But in one way Edith Gordon had been right;
if this ever got back to little Mike, when he was
old enough to understand its implications. . . .

Peggy decided, finally, that she would tell
Bill. She couldn't fight it alone, and it had to be
fought.

CHAPTER THIRTEEN

EARL ARRIVED first. She was in the kitchen preparing dinner and heard the door open and close. She went part way through the diningroom, then saw it was her brother instead of Bill, and went back.

Earl did not come to the kitchen for a long while. He was in there playing with the train again, and with Mike. She smiled a little, the first such effort since the Edith Gordon telephone call. What made her smile was that her brother, who habitually read his evening newspaper and refused to budge until he'd finished reading it, for the past two nights hadn't even opened the newspaper.

Finally, he strolled out, greeted her, and went to mix a couple of highballs at the sideboard. She said, "You can double up on mine tonight, Earl."

He looked at her, then turned back and didn't quite double up on it, but when she got the glass and tasted it, the noticeable bitterness suggested that he had indeed made it strong.

Then he went patiently to the kitchen table and, when he was comfortable there, he said, "Okay, somebody walked over your grave today. What's wrong?"

She turned slowly to face him and related exactly what had occurred without elaborating on any of it. He sat listening, looking stunned at first, then gradually getting that rusty-ruddy shade of dark red he got when he was truly angry. When she finished and turned back to getting dinner again, he said, "Have you told Bill any of this?"

Her answer was frank. "No and the reason I haven't is because . . . well . . . he might decide not to stay in Brunswick." She had her back to Earl and did not change stance. "And I don't want him to leave."

Earl tapped the tabletop with his fingers. She knew he was staring over at her. Eventually, he said, "Look, Peg, don't you suppose we ought to just get it all out into the open?"

She said, "Yes," still without turning. "I love him, Earl."

Her brother's chair groaned but she still did not look around. He'd shifted position. "Okay, you're in love with him. I'm glad for you; for *both* of you. But the next time he comes around . . . Is he coming over here tonight?"

"Yes. He said he'd be back. He went down to the Bellanger place to make some shelves for his law books, or something like that." Now, finally, she turned, and her brother was sitting over there, one arm over the back of his chair, his lean, handsome face creased into the expression of a man who had just bitten into something sour, staring stonily in her direction. His glass was empty; she'd hardly touched hers. "I'll tell him tonight," she said. "But if he goes away . . ."

Earl looked disgusted. "Goes away? Listen; answer one question for me. Have you told him you loved him?"

She nodded.

"By any chance did he tell you he loved you?"

She nodded again.

"Then what the hell kind of silly talk is this about him going away? A man in love with a woman doesn't just jump up, pack his shirts and socks, and run to the far end of the world because some silly, vicious old women started circulating lies about him no one's going to believe."

Earl was angry and disgusted. He sat there glaring at her. "And stop looking like a martyr, too," he growled.

She was surprised. She was also angered. They hadn't really quarrelled since childhood, but she felt very close to quarrelling with him right now. "I am *not* looking like a martyr!"

He suddenly smiled. "That's better. Now we can talk sensibly." He arose. "When Bill gets here I'll send him to the kitchen. Mike and I'll work out some routes with the train track. You tell him; mix him a drink first, then sit him down at the table, and you tell him. Okay?"

She nodded. "Okay."

Earl left the room, and Peggy went back to work getting dinner. Oddly enough, she felt much better, being angry at her brother seemed to have helped, somehow or other. Had he known that it would? Impossible; if there were a man on earth who knew nothing about women, it had to be Earl. But . . .

She heard the doorbell ring. Her heart sprang into her mouth. Moments later she heard Bill and her brother, then she turned, bracing for the moment when Bill came across the threshhold of the kitchen.

He must have stopped at the hotel because he looked immaculate and shiny-faced. He looked over at her and shook his head. "You know, Peg, I just can't imagine any situation where you wouldn't look like something out of a man's fondest dreams."

She smiled at him. "I think you are pretty, too."

He laughed. They met near the table, and she pushed him down into a chair. "Sit still while I make you a drink." He sat, and watched, and said nothing until she brought him the drink. Then she leaned upon the table for support and slowly, very carefully, told him about that earlier telephone call.

She got quite a shock. He sipped the highball slowly and looked up at her face now and then, but otherwise he showed hardly any emotion until she was finished. Then he softly said, "All right; I suppose something like this was inevitable, wasn't it? After all, I came here as a perfect stranger, started courting the prettiest girl in town, then showed up with a little child which I admitted belonged to me. We don't live in a world of spontaneous generation, do we—so, since I didn't bring along a wife, someone had to come up with this other tale."

She stared down at him. "You're not furious, Bill?"

He didn't smile. He finished the drink and put the glass aside. "I'm not exactly *happy,* sweetheart, but then you've got to remember that I've been a lawyer for some years now, and lawyers don't very often come across bluebirds of happiness." He kept gazing up at her. "I wish to hell it hadn't happened with you involved, Peg. People who live most of their lives in small communities aren't usually too well equipped for the bad aspects, are they?"

She sat down, trying to grope her way to a meeting of minds with him. "But—it's such a terrible thing to say about a little boy. About *you.*"

He reached out and held one of her hands. "Okay, but we can take care of that without too much trouble. What worries me is—you."

"Me?" she said. "How?"

"You don't know it's not true. Haven't you wondered, even once since that woman called, whether I actually have a wife or not?"

She shook her head at him in disbelief. "Not even once," she murmured. "You told me the story."

He squeezed her hand. "If you have that

much blind faith, then you don't have a thing to worry about. Tomorrow I'll go have a talk with Mrs. Gordon. I'll have to know where the story first started. After that it's a very simple matter of law, and believe me, I can handle it."

She kept watching his face. "Bill, did you honestly think I *believed* her?"

He returned her steady look. "Sweetheart, we're grown people; we only know one thing about each other. That we're in love. Most of the rest of it is a blank book, isn't it? How would I know how you think or what you think—beyond that one fact of love?"

He leaned and reached to bring her face close, then he brushed her lips, and as he leaned away, he said, "I think the potatoes are burning."

She sprang up. He was right. The potatoes were burning. She opened a window to let the smell escape, and the sudden rush of icy air that came in cooled her face as well as her thoughts. She decided, while standing at the window, that a storekeeper's sister in a village and a successful lawyer from a city like Burlington really *didn't* know how each other's minds worked.

He came over to help scrape the potato pan and in the process he nuzzled her neck. She turned aggressively and grabbed him, pulled him down to her, and pressed against him full length. She seared him with a kiss that was pure passion; then she turned loose and clung to him with her face pushed hard against his chest.

"What will you do?" she muttered.

"Right now?" he replied. "Just stand here until I can stop shaking."

She smiled against him in spite of herself. "No, you idiot. Not *now*. What will you do tomorrow when you go see Edith Gordon?"

"Explain to her that for slander and defamation of character she is now to be sued for one million dollars."

Peggy leaned back to look up at his face. "Bill . . . !"

He raised a hand to trace out the heavy, sweet lines of her lips. "Of course, I'm not going to sue her. But she won't know that, will she?"

"I can tell you where it started. At least, I'm fairly certain where it started. Remember when we talked long distance over the telephone and I told you I loved you? Well; it's been common knowledge around Brunswick ever since I can remember that the switchboard operators monitor most of the local calls; that's how folks keep up on the business and affairs of other folks."

He raised his fingers to her coppery hair, worked them deeply into it. "Fine. Sometimes individuals panic and go to pieces when they are faced with a lawsuit, but not corporations; they get very attentive and cooperative. Have you any idea which particular telephone operator might have been listening in?"

"No." Peggy wasn't even sure who worked for the telephone company any more. Years back she'd have known, but not now.

He smiled downward. "No matter. I'll find

out. Now listen, I'm either going to make wild and passionate love to you right here in the kitchen or you're going to have to feed me dinner. Which will it be?"

She did not drop her eyes but she blushed as she said, "How about dinner first . . . ?"

They heard some wide steps coming, accompanied by some shorter steps, and broke away. Peggy turned quickly to the sideboard and Bill went back over by the table. They looked perfectly normal when Earl and Bill's son came into the kitchen, except for the exceeding brightness of Peggy's eyes, which her brother noted impassively when she turned to explain about the burned potatoes and went to start setting the table for four diners.

Earl said, "You told Bill?" and when she nodded, her brother looked toward the other man, waiting.

Bill explained what he thought he would do, and as Earl listened it became evident to Peggy that *she* was the one who had almost been shattered into a hundred pieces, not the two men. They sat there quietly discussing that terrible thing as though they were planning a fishing trip.

But when Mike came over to her and looked up with his trusting expression, she could not help feeling as fierce as a mother eagle. *No* one, in Brunswick or any other place, was ever going to say *anything* that might hurt Michael Harland Tappan as long as she was within reach!

She perched Mike upon a stool and showed him how to shred lettuce for a salad, and gradually she decided that that terribly upsetting telephone call and its afternoon-long anguish had been resolved simply by having her brother and the man she loved in the kitchen with her this evening, along with the little boy she had loved from the first moment she laid eyes on him, now working very seriously beside her at the sideboard.

She stopped despising Edith Gordon and began pitying her, which meant that, at least for Peggy Wheaton, the first phase of their estrangement was over and the second phase would begin shortly, when Bill went calling tomorrow at the Gordon residence. Of just one thing Peggy was certain, right now, this evening: as long as she lived, she would never again be able to look into Edith Gordon's face and smile —and mean it.

CHAPTER FOURTEEN

SHE AWAKENED lazily the following morning thinking that she had, again, forgotten to mention that check. It was easy to justify such a faulty memory; after her brother had tactfully gone off to bed only about a half-hour after she and Bill had put Mike to bed, and she had been entirely alone with Bill before the fireplace on that cold, still, and quiet night. . . .

She rolled her body drowsily in the bed and closed her eyes briefly, with a soft-remembering smile around her lips. For a while she did not move, but eventually she got up, showered, dressed in jeans and sweater, pulled her dark, coppery hair into a girlish gather on both sides, tied it like that with two large pieces of brightly-colored yarn, and went out through the silent house to start breakfast.

She heard noise coming from the direction of Earl's room but not a sound from Mike's room. He had not gone to bed at eight, as he usually did, but had managed to elude the inevitable until almost nine o'clock. This morning he would probably sleep-in, not that she minded especially.

The coffee was bubbling, she had Earl's waffles ready, and was setting the table when her brother appeared. It was a cold morning but the sky was clear, which meant that some time today the sun would come. Usually, this late in the year, if there was much real warmth to the day it didn't arrive until about mid-afternoon, even though the sun had been out since early morning.

Her brother said something about the warmth melting the last of the snow from that freak storm, and she agreed. Then he said, "Bill's going to make arrangements with Helen Fairchild to baby-sit."

That was all he said until he'd eaten part of his first waffle. There wasn't much reason for him to say more anyway; Peggy already knew Bill had had something like that in mind. As for Helen Fairchild, she was a large, matronly, amiable soul whose husband had two trucks and did most of the local hauling between Brunswick and Buckner. Peggy had known them both most of her life. She had always liked Helen.

Earl finally said, "I suggested her. He asked if I knew anyone who did that kind of thing. Helen seemed the natural one."

She smiled her approval, which seemed to be what Earl was seeking. He finished breakfast and left, so she went to rouse Mike. When she

got to his room, he had already washed and
dressed but was having difficulty with a knotted
shoelace. She knelt, set that to rights, then took
him out and fed him.

Afterward he wanted to go out back, so she
made him bundle up first, and while he was
gazing upon the settling mound that had been
his snow-castle, she went to get his train from
the living room, where everyone had to step
over it going or coming, and put it in his
bedroom, next to the window where it would be
out of everyone's way, even Mike's, and where
he could play with it when he wished.

She cleaned house, too, not especially because
the place needed it but because she wanted to
keep busy. She knew that about now Bill would
be talking to Edith Gordon, and speculating
about that wasn't actually a good thing to do.

She expected him to come round about noon,
so all the while she was feeding his son and
afterward getting Mike to take his nap—and
not play with the train—she kept listening.

But the car did not arrive. In fact it was
mid-afternoon before he drove up, and by then
she was beginning to wonder.

She met him out on the porch. He kissed her
cheek, and when she would have taken him
indoors he hung back. It was delightfully warm
and pleasant this late in the day. The countryside
still looked cowed and brown after the storm,
but the air sparkled and those faraway hills
and peaks came across the distance as masterfully

sculpted works in very dark green and bright
white.

They went down off the porch and walked
over to the side of the house where an iron
bench stood. Peggy had always felt that the
bench, put there proudly by her father many
years ago, was more ornamental than practical;
it was the hardest thing to sit on she had ever
encountered, even harder than stone. But she
sat, and he sat beside her as he said, "Do you
know a girl named Florence Jones?"

Peggy had to pause and think. There were
two families in Brunswick named Jones. She
shrugged. "Not offhand. Why?"

"She's the eavesdropping switchboard operator," he replied.

"Edith Gordon told you that?"

"No, not exactly. Mrs. Gordon got part of her
story from Mrs. Jim Burley, and Mrs. Burley
got it from Florence Jones." He grinned at her.
"There seems to be a pretty fair intelligence
network here in Brunswick. Jones passed the
scoop to Burley, who enhanced it slightly to
impress Edith Gordon, then dropped it before
Gordon, with whom she evidently has some sort
of first-to-know competition going on. And
Edith Gordon added a little more embroidery
and passed it on among the lower echelon
gossips."

Peggy tried to place Florence Jones and
couldn't. The woman didn't actually have to be
related to the other Jones families in town

anyway; the name was common, and the telephone company had a large employment turnover. Florence Jones could be just some outsider who'd come to work for the telephone company in town.

She looked at Bill. "What was Mrs. Gordon's reaction when you talked to her this morning?"

He laughed a little in recollection. "Hostility, I'd say. At first anyway. She'd already begun believing her own gossip, I think. But after about an hour had passed and we'd got down to cases, she got so damned contrite and afraid I felt sorry for her. I went next to talk with Mrs. Burley. She almost fainted; she made me promise three times not to tell her husband. Then I went to see the officials at the telephone company."

"What does this Florence Jones look like?" Peggy asked, still puzzled by the woman's identity. But she got no help from Bill.

"I didn't see her. Didn't talk to her at all. I spoke to a woman named Burns, the assistant manager, and to a man named Gordon Hazlett, the manager. In fact Hazlett and I had lunch together at the hotel. He's a decent sort; it seems that if he didn't have only four years to go to his pension, he'd quit over the eavesdropping that goes on. He also told me he was going to fire Florence Jones this afternoon, and he was going to tell her exactly why he was firing her, and he would recommend that she come make her peace with me before she gets the hell sued out of her."

Bill threw up his hands. "That's the end of it, I hope."

Peggy wasn't that sure; she had thought quite a bit about that malicious gossip since getting Edith Gordon's telephone call, and her conclusion, based upon having lived all her life in a small town, was that gossip never really died, was never really forgotten by people, even though they might not mention it, normally. But she decided not to mention this, so she smiled and nodded, saying only, "I hope so." Then she arose. "You haven't had lunch, have you?"

He stood up too. "I just told you, Hazlett and I had lunch at the hotel. But I could drink a cup of coffee."

They went inside and back to the kitchen. She told him that Mike was napping, or at least she thought he was, and she also told him she'd put the train in Mike's bedroom and that the train seemed to compensate for the melting ruin out back that had been his snow-castle. Then, as she went about making a fresh pot of coffee, she remembered the check and turned suddenly.

He was sitting at the table, watching every move she made with a soft expression around his mouth and in his eyes. That temporarily disconcerted her, which gave him time to complete the diversion by saying, "I filed the divorce papers up in Burlington. Left everything in the hands of an old friend of mine, another lawyer.

He is going to expedite things, but no matter how fast those things go, in New England we're still going to be pilloried by the mandatory waiting period."

She didn't care. She didn't care that the way he had been looking at her when she turned so unexpectedly had been not just possessive. In any other man on earth she'd have resented that look fiercely, but in Bill she liked it, even wanted him to look at her like that.

She said, "I don't care," meaning she didn't care how long they'd have to wait before his divorce became final. She didn't care, either. She did not allow her thoughts to go beyond that statement, though. Inhibitions died hard, even in a woman in love. Perhaps in a *girl* in love they evaporated more swiftly and easily, but Peggy Wheaton had not considered herself a girl for several years. She was a woman.

He blushed. It was the first time she'd ever seen him do that. She grinned. "You're red in the face, Bill."

He looked away and back again before answering. "If you could have read my mind, you'd have been red in the face too."

She teased him. "Tell me, then."

He was almost adamant. "No way. How long do you allow coffee to perk, love?" He pointed. Behind her on the stove the cheery little sounds had been inaudible to her because of her concentration on him. She turned, shifted the pot to a cold burner, and turned back again. *This* time she was not going to be diverted.

"You were thinking terrible things—about us?"

He shook his head slowly. "Not terrible. Wonderful. Delightful, beautiful, ecstatic things." He kept looking at her. "When I was back in Burlington, I kept wondering—how the hell could I ever have made such an awful mistake years ago?"

She knew him, now, knew what he'd been like earlier. "Younger," she said, "more passionate and fiery, Bill?"

He nodded. "You're a mind reader. That's exactly what it was. All physical, like a couple of animals in springtime, Peg. I couldn't even force myself to make any kind of a comparison, but I came up with a gem of philosophical deduction: no one should be allowed to marry until the girl is twenty-one and the man is twenty-eight or twenty-nine."

She laughed. "If you could enact that into law, lover, you'd be lynched before you got home for dinner." She turned to get their coffee. "And anyway—suppose you'd come here three or four years ago? I was here, and I was just as big as I am now, and if we had struck fire then as we do now . . . ?" She didn't finish it, but when she took his cup over to the table and leaned down, she said, "Don't try to change the status of the world until you've changed the status of you and me."

She pulled away when his arms came up, went back and got the other cup, and returned with it to sit opposite him at the table. "What do we do while we're waiting for the divorce to become final?" She knew exactly what they would do, and actually it wasn't much different from what those younger people did that he'd just put down.

He tasted the coffee before answering. "In a city as large and crowded as Burlington, we'd probably live ecstatically in venial sin."

She nodded. "But this isn't Burlington, is it? We've just handled one dirty little mess of gossip. Do we start an even juicier bit of it?"

He looked at her. "I can't be around you and not want to do something that would start gossip."

She sighed. He wouldn't have to actually *do* anything at all. As time went on and they were together all the time, the gossip would just naturally start up all by itself. But she knew something about this particular kind of gossip: it ended and was eventually forgotten as soon as the people it was created around got married and became just another pair of settled, work-a-day members of the community. After that happened, the townspeople sought, and always were able to find, another pair of lovers to fix their thrill-hungry imaginations upon.

Maybe that wasn't bad; maybe it was natural and, in a way, maybe it meant that the older people were more interested in the younger people than just salaciously curious about them —and their morals.

And maybe, in ten or fifteen years, she'd be doing that same thing. She probably would because by then she'd have her own wonderful memories to relive in other young people. Maybe it wasn't bad at all.

CHAPTER FIFTEEN

THE NEXT day they got Helen Fairchild over early so that Peggy could explain about how to look after Mike, and Peggy got her first hint that the talk was already in progress.

Helen, who was a jovial, heavy, actually rather attractive woman with a creamy complexion and a warm, tolerant nature, said, "How long will you be gone; I expect you'll be over on Elm Street working on the Bellanger place, won't you?"

Helen only said that to make certain where she could contact Peggy if she had to, but it was a revelation in itself.

Later, as they were driving away, Peggy told Bill and smiled a little ruefully at him. He accepted it as a natural condition, the way he had accepted the Edith Gordon affair, and as they drove down through town in the crisp, golden morning, she settled back comfortably, thinking that he was a perfect partner for her. Whether others realized it or not, calm, predictable Peggy Wheaton was a person of sensitivity and quick, practical perception; it never took an awful lot to make her worry.

Bill did not worry very much, and even when he did, he kept it so well submerged that others did not suspect, which was a good way to be because worrying only caused others to worry, and when the crises passed, as they always seemed to do, the little interior scars were left, and *they*, never the crises, were damaging.

As they drove past the store, he said, "If people are talking about us, love, then they're leaving someone else alone. Anyway, from the people I've met so far around here, excepting only perhaps four or five, there really aren't any malicious ones." He turned. "Are there?"

She didn't try to count them. She thought he was right anyway, so she smiled and shook her head. "I'm glad you like Brunswick, Bill, because if you didn't . . . I suppose I'd wither up and die."

He had to watch the road until they swung over onto Elm Street, which rarely had much traffic, even in the evenings, before he could look at her again. "Brunswick is you, lover, and you are Brunswick. I couldn't very well love one without feeling something special for the other."

They drove up onto the old-fashioned twin ribbons of cracked cement that was the driveway, left the car, and as Peggy got out, it all rushed back at her from over the years: the big old apple tree out back, the meticulously-maintained white trim around all the windows and doors, the carefully-oiled wooden siding, and the sol-dier-like rank of pickets on the little fence out

front. She looked at the front of the house, half
expecting old John Bellanger to step out and
tell her to come in by the fire because it was
cold out there.

But of course he didn't come out.

She also remembered going for that long walk
on the evening of the day she had learned that
John Bellanger had died, and now, in thinking
back to that, she wondered if her compulsion to
get out under the sky that night hadn't perhaps
been some dumb-brute instinctive urging from
eons ago, when people had perhaps been able to
stand in a clearing somewhere and have a last
quiet talk with departing spirits.

Bill said, "Hey," and she roused herself to go
to the front door with him. The moment he
swung the door inward, she smelled paint and
knew that he'd already been at work here.

He reminded her of Mike, the way he took
her through and showed her where he'd painted
the small rear bedroom. "For Mike," he announced. She smiled at his pride, at his expression
of anticipation. She dutifully admired his choice
of colors and his workmanship. Both actually
were very good, but she was learning something
about men, too; they really *weren't* all that
different from little boys.

He showed her where he'd made plans to
have a study built on at the rear of the house.
He'd also planned on enlarging the main bedroom,
which actually was a bit small for two people
and a large bed. Then he took her to the
kitchen, which she remembered very well and

which she also remembered wondering about, even as a small child; people hadn't cooked on wood-burning stoves since she could remember, but John Bellanger had.

"Modernize it from wall to wall," he announced, making a wide-sweeping gesture with both arms. "You tell me what you want, and it shall be done."

In the living room, which John Bellanger had always referred to as the "parlor," there actually wasn't much that had to be done, except for fresh paint, some woodwork to replace, and refinishing the floor.

He wanted her advice. At first she gave it sparingly because she thought he had already made up his mind and she did not want any conflict. She could have lived in the house with him and his son just as it was—wood stove and all—and been wonderfully happy. But that wasn't what he wanted.

They spent more than an hour just wandering from room to room discussing wallpaper, colors, combinations of colors, and finally when they returned to the kitchen she got the idea that she was being handled with warm and affectionate tact; she hadn't said much when they'd been in the kitchen earlier, so he'd led her everywhere else, then maneuvered her back there. This time when he mentioned modernizing the kitchen, she pointed out where she thought a refrigerator ought to go and where the range and table would look best, and when she looked around, he was listening intently as though each thing she said were something he meant to remember very carefully.

She dropped her arm and laughed at him. She said, "Why didn't I tell you I loved you right from the start?"

He blinked. Modernizing a kitchen, to a man's way of thinking, was about as alien a subject to love as anyone could imagine. They were different; she dwelt momentarily upon that. They were different in all the ways that would make them one. She didn't try explaining *that* to him, either, any more than she tried to explain what she had meant just now when she'd said she should have told him she loved him earlier. He would never understand the connection between modernizing a kitchen and her wanting to tell him how much she loved him.

But it was really very simple; she loved him because he had maneuvered her so expertly back to the kitchen, and of course the reason he had done that was because he wanted her happy and contented when they finally could live here, and that meant, basically, that he loved her. It made absolute sense to her, but he'd just blinked, so now she said, "I don't want to wait six months or a year," and that, finally, found a response in him.

He looked steadily at her. "Neither do I." She saw the sudden hot willfulness appear in his eyes and also saw it begin to ebb just before he said, "I think we're caught in the web of the very same traditionalist hidebound morality we both like about this community, though. It'd ruin your reputation to move in with me now, and it'd ruin Mike's chances of making a go of it in school here, wouldn't it?" He smiled at her.

It would also ruin something else he hadn't mentioned; it would destroy his chances of becoming a respected attorney. In a town like Brunswick people historically and traditionally respected professional people. The citizenry was orderly and mostly law-abiding, everyone she could think of, and they expected, even demanded that much, and even more, from the professional people among them.

She said, "What's the answer, Bill?"

He could have said clandestine meetings, but she didn't expect that, and he didn't say it. "How do you like the word—discipline?" he asked, going up a step closer to her but not raising his arms as she ached for him to do.

"Truthfully?" she asked, and then answered before he could nod. "I *don't* like it . . . But I'll do it." She moved impulsively up against him. "Discipline isn't the same as abstinence, is it?"

He didn't answer for a long time because she raised a hand to draw his face down to her. She kissed him, then moved her mouth under his lips and continued to kiss him in that savage way she had been doing lately and which had originally shocked—even horrified—her to find that this kind of fierce, almost savage fire was inherently part of her.

When he got free he leaned into her a little limply. "There ought to be a law," he whispered.

She said, "Against this?"

"Hell, no. Against there being anyone else in the world when you do that."

She laughed against his shoulder. "Discipline, remember?"

"Yeah," he muttered huskily. "I can *remember*; the question is—can I do it and keep on doing it."

She took him back into the living room by the hand. "I didn't bring anything to put over my hair while we're painting," she said, and gave his fingers a savage squeeze, then released them and went over to lean at the front windows gazing out upon the golden, sparkling countryside visible from the far north end of Elm Street.

"How many children will we send from here over to the Poplar Street School," she mused aloud, without turning to look back where he was standing.

"Two boys and two girls," he said.

She turned. "In that case I suppose we'd better get busy with the painting hadn't we?"

He gazed at her with that same momentarily blank expression again, and then he said, "I suppose so."

She wanted to laugh. Maybe she'd never been a fast thinker, but somehow or other she was certainly thinking faster than he was, at least today; obviously, if they were going to start a family as soon as they respectably could, they should have everything ready, and the only way to accomplish that was by starting right now to get things ready.

He had buckets of paint and tools in the master bedroom, on a kind of improvised trestle-table. They went in there, and she wished again she'd brought something to protect her hair, until he said, "We can't really do much painting until the carpenters are finished, can we? I mean, they'll be stirring up an awful lot of dust."

She was agreeable; she hadn't really come prepared. "Then let's go for a drive into the hills," she suggested.

They went back out to the car, and instead of turning right, back in the direction of the center of town, they turned left toward the open, farming countryside beyond and, a number of miles farther, toward the great lift and sweep of the northeast to southwest curving of the far hillsides.

Something that was occuring, that occurred every autumn, still fascinated Peggy now, fifteen years later, as it had fascinated her when she'd been a child. Leaves turned all the wonderfully riotous colors of the rainbow in autumn, and they cascaded downward to form a carpet of magic scent and sound; but only after the first storm did the more stubbornly adhering ones finally relinquish their grip. She thought the frost somehow "set" them, and as long as the frost kept them congealed, they could not drop. But after a lot of frost, when the temperature suddenly zoomed back up again on a few Indian summer afternoons and everything, but particularly the frost-bound leaves, became

suddenly limp with warmth, they let go and
fell.

That was what was happening now; along the
tree-lined north roadway from town, leaves
rattled down all over the car and roadway.
They were crisp, dried out, and not as pretty as
they had once been because now they were
simply russet-brown, but they had a fragrance
that tainted everything, a kind of smoky, wonderfully incense-scented aroma that could only
be found in nature at this very particular time
of year.

She loved it—the sight of them falling, the
view up ahead on the arrow-straight roadway
as far as she could see, where leaves lay like a
tawny carpet—and she loved the wonderfully
gamey, strangely-stirring fragrance.

She also loved the man beside her, so she slid
closer until they touched at hip and shoulder
and put her head upon his shoulder.

She didn't care, right then, who they met or
even if they met the whole town of Brunswick.
Discipline? That would commence tomorrow!

CHAPTER SIXTEEN

THEY PASSED the storm-browned fields, passed puddles of slush in the old paved roadway. Passed farmhouses with thin gray fingers of smoke standing straight up into the warm, fragrant afternoon from curing-houses and kitchen chimneys. Once, at a particularly fine example of an old New England farmhouse he pointed and said, "Two hundred years old if it's a day," and she smiled because that was the old Burley place and that house had been standing more than two hundred years.

Nothing really changed very much around Brunswick except the people, she thought, and kept her head upon his shoulder. Someday, without much doubt, things would change, though. Whether for better or for worse people would have to decide when the changes arrived. Her children, she thought, would have to decide. But of one thing she was certain: whatever morals and values might come to replace the current ones around Brunswick township, they would come slowly, would meet stubborn Yankee opposition, and even if they triumphed, at least her children would have known what the old way was like.

A great doe sprang startled from the roadside, and although Bill was not driving fast, he had to apply the brakes sharply to avoid hitting the deer.

The doe suddenly stopped directly in front of the car. For a long moment Peggy and Bill were looking the graceful animal in the eyes. Then the doe gave another big bound and landed upon the far side where a post-and-rider fence stood. She cleared it without any effort and with her little tail erect, she galloped on out a few dozen yards before stopping again and turning with an expression of less surprise than indignation.

Bill recovered first from being thrown forward. He dropped back, looked round to see that Peggy was uninjured, and then he stared out where the doe stood and said, "She's beautiful."

Peggy agreed, once the shock was past and she could settle back again. "She's also an idiot to wait until the very last moment to try and cross the road."

Bill looked at Peggy, then laughed. She wasn't angry but she *had* been shaken, and that made her give that sharp comment. When he laughed she looked up ruefully at him. They drove on, leaving the doe to her thoughts.

Eventually, where the road began to rise a little from the flat farmland, the countryside did not look quite so thrifty, quite so man-managed and manicured. There were stands of scrub trees and thickets of underbrush. There were also more birds, and different kinds than were usually seen back in town. Up here, where nature had her first lines, there was ample sign to prove that man came here often, but the farther up they drove, the less sign of this intrusion there was until, eventually, where they began turning southwest around the massive haunch of a sidehill, the forest seemed determined to close out everything below and back down across the countryside as far as Brunswick. Up there, it was as though this was all virgin country, except for that winding, climbing road.

Once, when they stopped to watch some busy, small, striped rodents, he asked if she had any idea where the road would take them. She knew exactly where it would take them because she'd been making this trip one way or another for years.

"Monument Lake, about three miles on ahead."

He drove ahead, without asking where, exactly, or what Monument Lake was, beyond being a large body of water. But shortly before they got there he did say, "Like Miller's pond?"

There was no comparison, but all she told him was to be patient another mile or so, and he would see for himself.

When they reached it, the sunshine was just slightly beyond the meridian. Slanting golden light was over the lake and the tall-standing ranks of mighty pine and fir trees that almost entirely surrounded it. Where they left the car to walk forward there was a grassy clearing, still with about four inches of snow upon it at this elevation. The air was glass-clear and not as warm as it had been down around Brunswick.

He walked down to the shore with her and stopped to make a long study of Monument Lake. "Beautiful," he said quietly. "Soul-stirring."

"Come up again next summer during trout season," she told him. "It'll look very different then with boats all over it and campers up and down both sides."

He looked at her. "Dolly Varden?"

"What?"

"What kind of fish, Dolly Varden trout?"

"Oh, I'm not sure. You'd have to ask Earl, he's the fisherman in the family. That is, when he can get away from the store. They're trout, that's all I can tell you. One trout looks like the next one to me."

"I'll educate you," he said, and pulled her along by the hand as he started out briskly to explore the northeasterly shoreline.

If she'd thought to bring along a jacket, she'd have enjoyed it more, but when they'd left the house she hadn't even thought of Monument Lake. Finally, though, after following him for a hundred yards through shoreline sunshine, she was warm enough.

He stopped a couple of times at the water's edge and peered downward, but she wasn't really certain what this presaged until he finally slipped out upon a narrow spit of land. Then he pointed, as fat fish lying just below the

surface where the water was warmest suddenly
stirred at the overhead shadows. "Rainbows,"
he said, triumphantly. "German browns. I can't
make out the others." He looked at her. "We'll
come up here next spring as soon as the season
opens. Do you like to fish?"

She knew that a fate worse than death lay
just ahead, the moment she admitted that
although she'd been going fishing for years,
usually with John Bellanger, she really was not
a very good fisherman nor a very ardent one. So
she looked up smiling and nodding and also
hoping that he wouldn't really pin her down.

He didn't. He just leaned and kissed her
cheek, then her neck, and said, "I knew it, Peg.
I knew it the moment I met you back there
beside the Buckner road; you were put here to
wait for me."

She wouldn't ever have argued about that,
but if her willingness to go trout fishing with
him were the secret clue that confirmed this for
him, then she thought that they did indeed get
their celestial signs from entirely different
quarters.

She showed him where someone, no one knew
who since it had all happened so long ago, had
once built a stone and log house with one fairly
large, low-ceilinged room. The local legend said
the builder had been a Revolutionary War spy
who had helped the British forces and who
otherwise had lived up here alone and apart
from everyone else so that he could come and go
through the mountains and valleys without

anyone wondering. She also told him that the trouble with this romantic notion was that there had been no battles anywhere near Brunswick, and although a lot of German mercenaries had been garrisoned in the town for a year or two—and were the ancestors of quite a few Brunswickers in the village and out across the countryside although every German name had long since been Anglicized—a spy would have to have been an idiot to reside this close to a garrisoned town.

Bill went inside, examined the hand stonework, came back, and invited her in to see some initials he'd uncovered and a date—1799—but she refused to go inside.

"There are bats and spiders and the Lord knows what in that place," she said. "I'll take your word for the date and initials."

They went down to the sloping shoreline directly in front of the ancient cabin. Bill pointed to some underwater stonework. "Boat landing," he announced. "Mostly crumbled away, but I'd bet money that's what it was."

She could at least confirm this. "John Bellanger told me one time the Indians used to canoe over from the far shore and tie up here and trade with the last people who lived up here."

They left the old cabin and went onward another mile before he finally found a clearing and took her to the sunniest part of it where they could sit upon a warm old deadfall pine tree that had once been huge. She had to jump up a little to get seated.

He said, "What a place for a honeymoon," and she looked at him with a very faint frown.

"Here?"

"With a good tent, a stove, a sleeping bag, a canoe for fishing at dawn and just before dusk." He looked upward at the stiff-topped pines, and then he suddenly lowered his head.

"Well, for two or three days, before we go on a real honeymoon?"

But she had already decided there really wasn't anything basically wrong with the idea; it just took a little getting used to. Her idea of a honeymoon, for some inexplicable reason, had always been staying at a hotel in up-state New York, somewhere in the vicinity of Niagara Falls. That's usually where honeymooners went, wasn't it? At least traditionalist honeymooners.

But the more she dwelled on this other idea, the more it appealed to her. They would be completely alone, entirely free to do and to dress and to act exactly as they felt like. In fact, as they sat there completely separate from all the rest of the world, with warm sunlight on them, with the solitude and the forest fragrance on all sides, it was possible for her to feel something, at least to begin to feel something she had never felt before—a strangely wonderful detachment from everything she had ever been before, a kind of individualness that set her entirely apart from everything and everyone, except the soft-eyed, handsome man at her side.

She slumped in the wonderful warmth and said, "Woodland nymphs, Bill?"

He turned, laughing. "That's pretty close, I suppose. I'd have said free souls. At least for as long as we'd dare to be free souls."

"And Mike?"

"Mrs. Fairchild can look after him. This is just for you and me."

A thought came so suddenly that Peggy jerked up straight on the warm old log. "Incidentally—and don't interrupt this time—about that check you left in the note before you went to Burlington. It was too much, and I absolutely could not take it anyway."

He didn't say a word, so she looked around at him. His eyes twinkled. "Safe to interrupt now?"

She thought a moment, then said, "No. Not yet." But she'd said everything there was to say, so she sat there until she could almost feel him laughing although he wasn't making a sound, and finally, struggling to keep a straight face because she even wanted to laugh herself, she said, "All right. But don't argue with me about this, will you?"

He didn't argue and he somehow controlled the laughter. "Sweetheart, Mike loves you, and I love you. You know that, don't you?"

She nodded.

"Well then which would you rather have, an expensive gift each month or a check?"

She looked up. "You're starting an argument."

He looked around. "Here, in this perfect setting? With you? Never."

She thought of something. "I'll compromise."

He waited. "Fine. That's what lawyers like best. What kind of a compromise?"

"Put it in a bank account for Mike," she said. "Until we're married and I'm legally his mother. Shouldn't that give him at least a fair start at college, or something that he wants to do, someday?"

He kept gazing at her. Finally, he reached to touch her, but she knew this much about Bill Tappan: when he was moved, if she didn't get completely out of reach, the world exploded, the sky burned brighter, the distances shrank, and everything became something she could only describe as inner, and outer, starfire.

She jumped down off their log and went out a yard or two, then turned. "If we don't get back soon it'll be too late for me to start supper," and when his face fell, she laughed. "I don't really want to be that practical. But one of us has to be, don't you agree?"

He stepped down and shoved his hands in his pockets, imitating a sulking little boy, and walked over to her. When she laughed, he took her by the hand and they started back together.

She was absolutely certain there was not another man like him anywhere upon the face of the earth. And of course, that was how she had to think, to be what she already was to him, and what he already was to her.

CHAPTER SEVENTEEN

WHEN THEY got back and he took her to the front door, the sun was gone and dusk, which hardly arrived at all in autumn and winter, was already yielding to swift-falling night.

He came in only briefly, then left, and Earl shook his head about that, but Peggy defended him. "He's very conscious of spending so much time here and of feeling under some kind of obligation to us for keeping Mike. Earl, this isn't a very easy time for him."

Earl thought that over, and whatever conclusion he arrived at, he kept to himself. He had been in Mike's bedroom when she'd got home. Later, when she went to get Mike for dinner, she discovered that the train track had been extended, had, in fact, been more than doubled and now covered two-thirds of the bedroom floor. Also, there was a stony tunnel the train had to pass through and several red and green signal-arms that were operated electrically when the train came near them. No wonder Earl had been in there. She took Mike back to the kitchen with her, wondering how long it would be before Mike and her brother began wearing those cloth-billed, striped hats the oldtime steam-engineers used to wear.

At dinner Earl casually mentioned that Elmer Shipman, Brunswick's best, but slowest, carpenter had come by the store for some hardware that afternoon. He was going to commence work at the John Bellanger place first thing in the morning.

"Shelf hangers," said Earl. "Cupboard hardware, latches, hinges, and the like. I'd say from the list Elmer had it's to be quite an alteration up there."

Peggy recognized the signs of curiosity in her brother. She didn't mind, so she told him how she and Bill had spent more than an hour. Earl listened, interested, and when she was finished, he and Mike discussed a new plan they had for re-routing the train track so that it would go over a gradual incline. She thought no more about what her brother had said until, more than an hour later when she was cleaning up the kitchen and thought Earl was in Mike's bedroom, he came ambling back to the kitchen doorway, and said, "Peg, when I took Helen Fairchild home this evening, she told me she thought Mike was just about the nicest-mannered little boy she had ever known."

Peggy turned. That was no secret. Mike *was* well-mannered. She said, "I'm glad Helen liked him."

Earl nodded as though dismissing this topic.

"She also got to talking about Bill. It wasn't too hard to figure out from the things she said that Bill's gotten to be something of a town topic."

"He's new here," she retorted. "Folks in town have always done that, Earl, talk about any newcomer who showed up."

"Yeah. But they're also talking about your association with him."

"Did Helen say that?"

"No. She didn't have to, Peg. When you've been in the store as long as I have, you get so that you just naturally guess what's behind the things people say, and Helen isn't subtle."

Peggy finished drying her hands and went to put some lotion on them, as she did every night. When she turned back, her brother was gazing patiently at her, so she said, "I don't know what to tell you, Earl. You already know I'm in love with him. What else can I say?"

He wasn't passing any judgments, evidently, because he said, "Nothing, I guess. Only you could do us all a favor if you were . . ."

She smiled without humor. "Discreet?"

He said, "Yeah, I suppose that's it."

She knew all about that. She'd seen other people try it over the years. It never succeeded. "Earl, even if we are discreet, it won't stop people from talking. And that's not necessarily bad, is it? Except for the kind of vicious talk Edith Gordon and her friends pass back and forth, I don't think people talk about Bill and me because they expect the worst or hope the worst will happen. I think they like to relive something, especially the older people; they aren't mean or dirty-minded, are they?"

Earl did not answer; he simply leaned there gazing at her and listening. He looked a little dubious but not altogether so. She may have just put forth an idea that he hadn't really considered before; there was no reason why he ever should have considered it, either. Earl Wheaton had never been the target of any gossip, at least as far as Earl and his sister knew, which was probably true because he'd led an entirely work-a-day, colorless life.

Mike appeared in the doorway, his face flushed. The train had stopped running and he wanted Earl to come and fix it. That ended the discussion. While Earl went back to the bedroom with Mike, Peggy went out back and stood upon the small rear porch for a moment in the star-filled cold night. It was beautiful out there, and except for the bitter cold she'd have remained longer.

Over where the westerly curve of the mountains shone ghostly pale in the moonlight, lay Monument Lake and the golden-drenched small, fragrant meadow where they'd sat in peace that afternoon. Someday they would go back up there and make a camp in that lovely place before the fishermen came or the hunters or anyone at all, and they'd live as free souls and do all the things lovers had to do in order to start creating their treasured memories.

Meanwhile, it seemed, they would have to

be—discreet—but even so, people were going to be interested in them. She smiled. If John Bellanger had been alive now, he'd have had some sound words of advice for her. But what could anyone say that she did not instinctively know?

Somehow, the time would pass, they would survive whatever ensued, and it was impossible for her to imagine herself ever feeling any different than she felt right now, had felt, in fact, for some time now. Maybe that was the purpose behind how she felt; perhaps the reason she had this feeling was so that it would cushion her over the wrenching transitions and adaptations she would have to make.

She studied the high sky. How could people believe there wasn't a reason, a genuine purpose? She said a little prayer, then turned back to get where the heat was. The night was so deathly still and clear the largest stars seemed almost within arms' reach.

If it had been warmer she'd have stayed out there longer, and perhaps if it had been one of those hot, wonderful summertime nights, she wouldn't have gone back indoors at all.

Earl was in the living room. She wondered about that and went to look in on Mike. He was already in bed, but evidently he hadn't been there very long because when she leaned to kiss him and lift the blankets closer around his shoulders, his face was still flushed. She opened one window a crack, then threaded her way carefully and silently, so as not to awaken him, back through the maze of railroad track to the door. Mike made a little puppy-sound and moved slightly in his sleep.

She went out to the living room. Earl looked over his newspaper at her. "I guess he finally got trained-out. He told me he wanted to go to bed." Earl smiled. "He's quite a little boy, Peg. You know, for no older than he is, that kid's as smart as a whip. You explain something that he can understand, and he remembers it; he even applies it where it fits. I doubt there are very many little kids that can pick things up like that and can retain them."

She smiled at her brother, with that same little stab of pain in her heart she'd felt the first time she'd watched Earl playing with Mike on the floor.

"I suppose it's unanimous, then," she replied. "You like him, Helen Fairchild likes him, I like him. Who does that leave?"

Earl had a ready answer. "Other little kids, Peg. We can't keep him cooped up all the time. If he's going to live in Brunswick, the sooner he gets to know the other little kids he'll be growing up with and going to school with, the better. It's hard on a boy to just walk in cold his first day at school."

She almost laughed. "Where did you learn so much about child-raising?"

Earl squirmed slightly as he replied. "A man doesn't have to read books about things like that. I've seen it happen right here in Brunswick over the years; a new kid comes to town, starts school, and he's got to prove himself just about every day or two. Mike shouldn't have to do that, should he?"

"No; and of course you're right. We'll have to start making plans, I guess."

Earl smiled as though he had just achieved a small triumph. "Thanksgiving is coming up, then Christmas. Everyone's pretty active during those holidays. You and Bill could show up at some of the socials—with Mike."

Obviously, this wasn't something her brother had just come up with on the spur of the moment. She said, very frankly, "Earl, sometimes you really surprise me. And I thought I knew you backwards and forwards."

He did not seem able to decide whether he liked that or not. "Nothing very damned complicated about seeing what a little kid needs, is there?" he growled, and flicked his newspaper, then ducked down behind it.

Peg had been knitting an Afghan; at least she had started one about a month ago, although she hadn't touched it, nor even thought about it, lately. Now she remembered it and went to get the basket with the balls of colored yarn, her needles, and as much of the Afghan as she'd already completed.

It was pleasant, using her hands, being busy in the quiet old house. Lately, those long interludes of tranquility which she'd begun rebeling against a month or two back, hadn't been possible, and now that one of them had arrived again, she didn't rebel against it at all but rather welcomed it and enjoyed it. She could knit and think at the same time.

But no matter where her plans and anticipations and even her dreams took her, they always came back to the same hard fact: nothing was really possible until Bill's divorce was final.

She had no idea how long people being divorced in Vermont were required to wait before their legal separation was pronounced final. For that matter, she didn't know how long a divorce took in Massachusetts or anywhere else, actually. She'd never thought about divorces, except in an offhand, saddened way. And she most certainly had never, not even in her most bitterly rebelious moods, ever thought of going with a married man or of ever wanting to marry a man who had been married and divorced.

She had somewhere, along the road to maturity, acquired a feeling of disapproval of divorced people. She certainly hadn't got it from Earl, who never said much one way or the other about such things, and as well as she could remember, her mother hadn't said anything derogatory about divorced people. But somewhere she'd acquired it because as she sat there, warm and relaxed and comfortable, she had the disapproving thoughts in the back of her mind.

She heard Mike cough and lowered the knitting needles to listen. It was a deep cough, not just one of those light, rasping little throaty coughs. She waited a minute, and when he coughed again, she looked over at Earl, but he was too engrossed in his newspaper to have heard the sound, or to at least have heeded it.

She put down her needles and got to her feet. Earl looked up. "Going to bed?"

"Mike's coughing," she said, and started toward the bedroom.

Earl called after her. "You're acting just like a mother. Everybody coughs."

She went to Mike's door, opened it slightly and peered toward the bed in the dim light. By the faint starlight, she could see the small mound in the center of the big old bed. She could also hear the labored breathing. For a moment she almost panicked. Then she entered the room, remembering the little flushed face. It also suddenly occurred to her that what Earl had attached no significance to, Mike wanting to go to bed, hadn't been just the wish of a tired child.

She went forward, leaned, put a cool palm upon the child's forehead, and felt the fever burn into her hand with a steady heat.

She went back swiftly and got her brother. They returned together, and this time they turned on the light. Earl took a long look, then pulled back and said, "We've got to have Doc Benton right away, Peg. You stay here and I'll go make the telephone call."

She sank down upon the bed with a feeling of helplessness deeper and more totally immobilizing than any other feeling she'd ever had in her life.

CHAPTER EIGHTEEN

DOCTOR RALPH Benton had been in semi-retirement ever since Peggy and her brother could remember. In fact, it had been a joke around Brunswick township, particularly when folks saw Ralph Benton's dusty car go whipping out of town, that for a man who was supposed to be in retirement, or at least semi-retirement, Doc Benton worked harder than most of the un-retired merchants around town.

Doctor Benton did not look any older now, either, than when he had come by to set Earl's broken arm fifteen years ago. He was a wiry, brown-skinned, sharp-eyed man with a mane of grizzled gray hair and dark-rimmed glasses. He was jovial almost any time, except when he was in a sick room, as he now was, and even then, although he did not say much, he could convey hope and confidence just by the way he looked at Peggy and smiled.

"When you were small," he said, "things like this didn't respond too well to what we had, and when your parents and I were children, it was much worse."

Doctor Benton leaned over the bed, before anyone could press him for whatever he hadn't finished saying, and resumed his examination. Little Mike did not seem to care at all that a total stranger was bending over him. Peggy's hands were damp from clasping them tightly. She knew Earl was looking at her, so eventually she tore her eyes away from the bed and half turned toward him.

"One of us ought to call Bill," he said. She had thought of this earlier, while she'd been soothing the feverish child during the wait for Doctor Benton.

She said, "Will you do it?"

Earl went silently out of the room.

Doctor Benton straightened up, looked with a squinted glance at the overhead light, and said, "Suppose you turn that off, Peggy, and use only the little lamp on the dresser. Right now the lad doesn't need a bright light in his eyes."

She moved to obey at once and turned back only when Doctor Benton was resuming his examination. In the more subdued lighting he seemed to take an inordinate length of time. To Peggy, at least, it seemed that way, but what Ralph Benton was doing was making several different confirmatory tests. He knew what Mike Tappan's trouble was, but he was an excellent diagnostician as well as a successful general practitioner because he never made snap-judgments. He was not just methodical, he was absolutely sure before he started treatment.

Eventually, he straightened up, and when Mike's listless gaze rose to his face, Doctor Benton said, "Well, son, I suppose it's just that time of year again, isn't it? Spring and autumn; that's when we get it." He smiled, caught the child's limp wrist, watched the sweep-hand of his wristwatch again, and when Peggy thought he would never stop taking that pulse, he looked at her over the dark, thick rim of his glasses.

"If you don't quiet down, girl, I'll have to treat you too."

Earl returned to the doorway and Doctor Benton said, "Get your sister a cup of coffee with some brandy in it, Earl. She's working herself into a state of nervous ruin."

Peggy shook her head. "I don't need that."

Doc Benton placed the hot, small arm back upon the blankets. "Where is the lad's father? Isn't this child the son of that new lawyer in town?"

Earl nodded. "Bill Tappan is his name, Doc. I just called him at the hotel. He'll be right along. What's wrong with the child?"

Doctor Benton moved back by the window and leaned to close it completely. "Lots of different names for it, Earl, but it's congestion of the chest. As I just said, we get most of it when there are drastic changes in the weather. From hot to cold and from cold to hot. In springtime they used to call it croup, and in the autumn it was always influenza, or something like that."

Peggy's brow creased. "But I wrap him up before I let him go outside to play, Doctor."

Ralph Benton was sympathetic. "Sure you do, Peg. This isn't anything you can take credit for; I've already had at least fifteen cases so far since that freak storm, and before winter sets in good and it stays cold day and night, I'll have another fifteen. Anyway, I can dose him with antibiotics, which we didn't have when I was his age.

"I'll keep him under treatment, but you've got to do most of it. He's absolutely under no circumstances to go outside or be in a draft or get out of bed and scamper round the house— or play on the floor with that electric train. You keep him well fed, Peg, but not *over*-fed, do you understand? Don't abide by that old saying about feeding a cold and starving a fever. Keep him well-nourished, no more and no less."

Doctor Benton went over to rummage for a hypodermic syringe in his satchel and load it, with his back to Peggy and Earl, with some thick, white fluid. When he turned around he said, "Medicine is wonderful. It's a help we'd all die a lot sooner without, but the *real* treatment lies with you. And when the fever breaks, you're going to have the devil's own time of it keeping him in bed. Just remember, he'll probably recover in spite of you and me and the antibiotics, but how *soon* he'll recover rests largely with you."

Doctor Benton went over to the bed, scrubbed the small arm, maneuvered so that Peggy's view was blocked by his back, and inserted the needle. She saw Mike's eyelids flicker, but that was all. She wanted him to cry out or to struggle, but he did neither. When Doctor Benton afterward massaged the arm and smiled, the child looked reproachfully at him, and the physician chuckled.

"You're fine. You'll come out of this in ten days or I'll buy you more track for the train. You're pretty tough, and I like that in a little boy."

Doctor Benton was putting things back into his satchel when the doorbell rang out front. Earl turned and left the room.

When Bill walked in he looked white. He hadn't even put on a coat over his jacket, and when Peggy introduced him to Ralph Benton, the doctor seemed to notice this because he said, "Be calm, Mr. Tappan. The boy's got a congested chest; maybe it'll only settle into a bad cold and maybe it'll go into something more serious. But you aren't going to help him any by jumping out of a warm bed and rushing up here without a scarf and hat and jacket."

Bill went over and sat on the edge of the bed. Little Mike's listless fingers worked into his father's palm. Bill closed his hand gently around them, and Peggy felt the tears stinging her eyes.

Doctor Benton was the only one in the room who could hold the balance, and he did it with soft-spoken, calm words. He repeated what he'd told Peggy, for Bill's benefit, then he said, "Let him sleep all he wants to. If you visit him, Mr. Tappan, do it early in the morning, right after he's had a good night's rest. Otherwise, do him a favor and leave him in the hands of Miss Wheaton. And now I've got to get along."

Bill looked around quickly. "Prescription, Doctor . . . ?"

Ralph Benton paused in the doorway. "Tender loving care until tomorrow, Mr. Tappan. I'll be back about ten or eleven in the morning." He jerked his head for Earl to go out to the front door with him. When they were gone, Peggy went over to Bill.

"We shouldn't have left him today."

Bill looked up at her. "You're not blaming yourself, are you? It wasn't anyone's fault, Peg. The most important thing is that he'll be all right in a few days." He pulled her down next to him on the bed and put his son's hot, small hand into her hand. Then he closed his larger hand over them both, and he smiled. There was a little color back in his face.

She wanted to cry; not for little Mike, not this time, but for some other reason that she wasn't exactly sure about.

She knew how much his son meant to him. In

the midst of her anguish, a sudden terrifying thought occurred to her. This time, while his son was in her care, he would recover, she was sure of that because Doctor Benton never told anything but the absolute truth to people, but the next time . . .

She suddenly let it burst out of her. "I'm afraid, Bill."

"You heard what the doctor said, Peg."

"I don't mean that. I heard, and I know he's going to be all right *this* time. I'm terribly afraid of the responsibility. . . . What about the next time and maybe the time after that?"

His hand tightened suddenly over her hand. "You're letting your imagination run away with you, sweetheart."

"But—something terrible could happen."

"No. Not with both of us looking out for him. But even if it did—like it happened this time, Peg—it's no one's fault."

Earl returned, looked at them, then silently withdrew in the direction of the kitchen to make a fresh pot of coffee. He had hardly said a word since Doctor Benton had arrived, and even before that, except for making those two telephone calls, he had said very little. Earl was one of those people in whom a crisis produced deep thought and long silences.

Mike fell into a deep slumber, which was probably the best thing for him right then, but the sound of his bubbly, hard breathing tore at Peggy. She stood up, carefully, so as not to awaken the child, and went past the dresser with its mirror on her way to the windows to make certain they were all tightly closed against the bitter cold. She was shocked at her face in the mirror. The only color was the deep, dark dullness of her eyes.

She turned after making sure of each window and said, "If you and Earl will lend a hand, I'll move a cot we have upstairs down here to his room."

Bill rose as though he might protest. Then he simply nodded and followed her to the doorway, out into the hall beyond, and they met Earl in the entry-way. He beckoned and led off to the kitchen. There, they did not have to be quiet, but Earl handed them both a cup of black, hot coffee, and until Peggy tasted hers, she had forgotten what Doctor Benton had said about brandy. There was a very generous jolt of liquor in the coffee. She drank it although she did not really like the taste of liquor, and moments later she could feel muscles relaxing, nerves retracting, warmth pushing upward from the locality of her stomach, and when Earl finally spoke, she went to the table and sank down there to listen.

"I'll admit I was afraid a half-hour ago, but now I'm beginning to feel better." He looked from Peggy to Bill. "Don't worry about Doc Benton; he may look like a horse-and-buggy practitioner, but I can tell you from seeing him work all my life that he's one of the best.".

Bill drank his laced coffee and nodded at

Earl; then he looked at Peggy, troubled and anxious. Earl must have guessed his thoughts because he spoke again, the second time.

"She'll be all right. Her trouble is that she's always been mothering something, a kitten, a bird, a stray puppy, something, ever since I can remember, and now she's got a little boy to fret over."

Peggy drank more of the coffee and stared at her brother. Within the past two weeks she had got to know Earl better than she had known him in all the preceding long, and sometimes troubled, years.

He was wonderful. She finished the coffee, leaned forward, put her head upon her arms atop the table, and cried, finally.

The men stood stock-still, watching. Finally, Bill put his cup aside and started forward. Earl reached out, caught an arm, and when Bill looked up, Earl shook his head and led the way out of the kitchen into the diningroom. He took Bill all the way back to the entry-hall, where they halted at the entrance to the lighted hallway. There, they could hear Mike's troubled but steady breathing.

"I guess you never had a sister," Earl told Bill Tappan. "I know; you think she needs someone to comfort her. Bill, I've been through this with her a hundred times since she was twelve years old. Take my word for it—leave her alone."

Bill stood unhappily. He could hear the sobs from the kitchen, faintly, and he could also hear the troubled breathing of his child. Even-

tually, he decided Earl knew what he was
talking about.

They went upstairs to get the cot and bring it
back down to put in Mike's room.

CHAPTER NINETEEN

THE FIRST night was the hardest. Mike awakened coughing and having trouble getting his breath. She was up and down with him until shortly after five o'clock, when he fell into a deep sleep. She did the same, and when she finally opened her eyes, the sun was shining in all the bedroom windows. It had to be at least nine o'clock; she got up, worrying about breakfast, drew the draperies to keep the room dim, tiptoed to her own room, showered, gargled with a strong mouth and throat wash, and got dressed. But when she reached the kitchen, there was only a cleaned plate and an empty coffee cup to show that Earl had got his own first meal of the day.

She drank some coffee, leaning upon the sink and looking out into the gorgeous new day, and when the doorbell rang, she ran to open it and tumble into Bill's arms.

He kissed her, entered, shoved the door closed with a heel, and held her at arms' length. She must not have looked as drawn and haggard as he had expected because he smiled and gave her a slight shake. Then he said, "How's the patient?"

"Sleeping. But come along and you can peek in at him."

They went soundlessly. She opened the bedroom door with great care, and Bill leaned across her to look toward the bed. Mike's small, flushed face was sideways on the pillow. He was still having trouble breathing, but evidently he was either too exhausted to be awakened by this or else he wasn't having as much trouble as he'd had the night before.

They moved back, eased the door closed silently, and went out into the entryway. Peggy said, "I think there's some improvement. Is that possible, just overnight?"

Bill did not really know. "He seems to be resting better and breathing a little easier."

She detected the subdued relief; he was controlling his hope, which she understood because she was doing the same thing. She took him to the kitchen, but he declined coffee and breakfast both. He had eaten at the hotel, he told her. Ten minutes later Doctor Benton arrived, and in a way Peggy regretted that; she didn't want Mike awakened. But Doctor Benton was a busy man so she only said that the child hadn't slept very well until about five o'clock, and Ralph Benton smiled as though he had expected this, which was mildly mystifying.

They returned to the bedroom. Doctor Benton awakened Mike by perching on the side of the bed and putting a broad, capable hand upon his forehead, then upon his throat, and finally, as the child opened heavy eyes, Doctor Benton raised his pajama top and put a stethoscope on Mike's chest as he'd done the previous night. He said nothing, did not even raise his eyes to Bill and Peggy.

He rolled the child up onto his side and put the stethoscope in several different places on Mike's back. As always, he was in no hurry. When he had pocketed the stethoscope, he made several raps here and there on the child, then went through the routine of taking his pulse and temperature.

Bill and Peggy stood like statues, which they could have been for all the attention Ralph Benton paid to them. He finally stood up and studied the little boy in long silence. Mike looked back, just as interested or curious, whichever it was, until Doc Benton seemed to conclude his private consultation and went to open his black bag.

"Some people," he said, finally, speaking as casually, as conversationally, as though they'd all been talking right along, "don't respond to antibiotics worth a hang. Others react, and with a small child that's always the biggest peril because we don't have any of the big-hospital equipment here to predetermine potential allergies. And then there are some people who respond very well to antibiotics. Usually, if we catch the patient quickly enough and if he is a favorable responder, we can pretty well inhibit the spread of an infectious ailment, something like—call it croup. That's not a popular name for what ails the lad any more, but I like it."

While he was discoursing, Doctor Benton was putting some small capsules from a larger bottle into a much smaller bottle. He did not look at Peggy or Bill, which was probably just as well because they exchanged an expression of annoyed impatience. Doctor Benton was taking a very long way around whatever he was leading up to.

"If a child reacts favorably," the doctor went on, as he counted out each capsule as though it were a gold nugget, "we can usually be thankful for two things: one, he has no allergy, and two, he has probably never had antibiotics before and therefore has no inherent built-in resistance to them."

Doctor Benton turned, holding out the small bottle to Peggy. "Mike is doing better, actually, than I had expected. No unfavorable reaction. The drugs are almost living up to their name— miracle drugs. Which, of course, they aren't, but right now you two would be willing to swear they are."

He smiled at them over the heavy rims of his glasses "I think, though, that we'll discontinue the injections. Those pills ought to do the trick as follow-up medication. Peg, I rarely ever make predictions, but I'll go out on a limb this morning and predict that the child will be trying to find excuses to get out of bed and play with his train by day after tomorrow. But," Doctor Benton held aloft a rigid finger. "But if you let him sit on that damned floor or leave that bed except to go to the bathroom for another four or five days, I'll personally come back and paddle you."

Bill relaxed all over. Peggy could sense it even though he was behind her and to one side of her. She wanted to do the same thing; in fact, she wanted to stretch out on the couch in the living room and close her eyes and not have to open them again for ten hours. But what she actually did was go out to the front door with the doctor. Bill started to come along, one hand reaching inside his jacket, but Doctor Benton waved that away.

"I'll send you a bill, Mr. Tappan. Never fear about that. But let's not rush things, eh?"

At the door Doctor Benton took one of Peggy's hands and clasped it tightly. "Girl; tonight let someone else stay up with him. Tonight, you get eight hours of sleep. You look like the wrath of God. I'll be back some time tomorrow. Oh, I almost forgot. Give the lad one of those pills a couple of hours before breakfast in the morning and another one a couple of hours before supper at night. I'll see you tomorrow." He released her hand, let himself out, closed the door, and she turned to find Bill standing in the hallway looking over at her. She smiled, and then she went over to him and raised her arms to his wide shoulders.

"What else can happen?"

He drew her close without smiling or without answering. She clung to him for a long time, eyes closed, body loose, feeling so terribly grateful to Someone. It never once occurred to her that Bill usually raised her face and kissed her when they were like this. She had finally let down, and all the tension, all the tiredness, all the built-up fear and dread left her gradually, until she was only conscious of the deliciousness of being held close while she slipped into a kind of thankful peace.

They were still standing like that moments later when Earl came up the outside steps. Peggy heard the familiar footfalls, pulled upright, looked from Bill to her wrist, then turned as her brother opened the door and stepped inside.

"It isn't even noon," she said, unable to remember when Earl had come home from the store before five o'clock.

Her brother shrugged and loosened his jacket. "How's the patient? I saw Doc driving up this way about an hour ago. There wasn't much doing at the store, so I thought I'd just take a little walk. You know, being in that store eight hours a day, a person really needs exercise. Well . . . ?"

They told him. Then they took him into the bedroom, but Mike was asleep again. Earl resisted Peggy's tug on the sleeve and cocked his head to listen to the child's breathing. Finally, he allowed himself to be taken to the living room.

He smiled at them and said, "I wasn't really worried. Not with Doc Benton handling things."

Peggy laughed softly. "No, I'm positive you

weren't. When was the last time you left the store in mid-day, Earl?"

Her brother looked at Bill. "That's something else about women," he said. "They're always looking for a devious motive in everything you do." He shed his jacket and tossed it upon a chair. "As long as I'm here, Peg, you might as well feed me."

They went back to the kitchen and she went searching through cupboards and the refrigerator. Only when she happened to turn, once, and caught Bill's profile did something suddenly jangle in the back-most portion of her mind. He had been so silent. She had thought that was because Doctor Benton had done most of the talking, earlier. But when he had held her in the entry-hall . . .

She almost said something. Instead, she decided to wait until Earl had had lunch and was gone.

She knew there was definitely something wrong when she put the meal before them. Bill, who was almost invariably a good eater, ate very little. He kept up his end of the running conversation her brother pursued through lunch, but although Earl seemed not to suspect that something was wrong, Peggy did.

Bill Tappan was one of those people who kept their troubles, their problems, mostly to themselves. She usually liked that in him, but right now she didn't.

Finally, Earl arose from the table. They went back into the living room with him until he had put on his jacket. He didn't button it, though, and when he thought his sister's gaze was some kind of silent reproach, he said, "It's almost sixty-five degrees out there."

He smiled at them. "That's one hell of a load off my mind," he said, as he trudged back to the front door and disappeared beyond it.

Peggy reached, turned Bill toward her, and held tightly to his upper arms. "Don't you feel well?" She asked. "You didn't eat, and you haven't acted the same since you walked in. Bill . . . ?"

He took her by one hand over to a window where sunshine was streaming in. He neither looked at her nor spoke. He dug in a jacket pocket, brought out a crumpled letter, and handed it to her.

She felt her stomach knotting the moment she saw the address on the upper left-hand corner of the envelope. It was from an attorney-at-law in Burlington, Vermont.

He turned, saw her hesitating, and said, "Read it."

She knew as well as she knew her own name it had to do with his wife. That knowledge was like a steel band around her heart.

It was hard to do, but very resolutely she removed the crisp paper, unfolded it, and read. The blow was almost physical at first. Then she reread the letter. She did not raise her eyes when she said, "Oh, Bill, I'm so terribly sorry."

He took the letter from her, put it back very carefully into its envelope, and pocketed it again. "That was waiting for me first thing this morning when I came downstairs at the hotel. That's why I didn't get up here until late."

The letter had only said rather stiffly that his wife had been drowned in France in a swimming mishap.

No one really had to have more details than that. Whatever else there was to tell about the tragedy wouldn't ameliorate anything, wouldn't be able to change anything.

Peggy seemed more shaken than Bill was. In fact, it was Bill who took her over to the couch by the fireplace and eased her down.

She had never known the woman, and if they had ever met, she had been certain she couldn't possibly have liked her. But death was so final; she hadn't encountered it very often in her lifetime, but each time she had, it had done something inside her, as it did now, as it had when John Bellanger had died and, much earlier, when her mother had died.

He sat beside her, held her hand, and for a long while there was nothing said. With death, there really *was* nothing to say. It arrived and it swept everything before it. It was the epitome of finality.

CHAPTER TWENTY

FOR PEGGY there was a saving grace: Mike. She sat with him a lot over the next couple of days, and when his father arrived, the three of them visited a little in his bedroom, like a family, as the child grew stronger.

Doctor Benton returned once again, on the third day, and reiterated his earlier warning about allowing the child out of bed too early. Then he left and did not come back, but Peggy thought of him a lot—each time the patient, who had nothing to do but lie there and think up excuses, tried to convince her he was well enough to get out of bed.

He tried that several times with his father, but there was a noticeable difference in the way he tried it, and Peggy was amused because, obviously, Mike thought he could outsmart her; but with Bill his approach was along the lines of plausible logic, as when he told his father that if the two of them played with the train on the floor, he could bundle up and keep a blanket under himself on the floor.

But it didn't work, and after a while when Peggy or his father grinned at his failures with them, Mike grinned back.

Earl visited the child each evening before dinner. Sometimes Peggy heard them spiritedly arguing in there as though they were both thirty—or as though they were both four-going-on-five. They had an excellent relationship, which pleased Peggy, of course, but it still surprised her because Earl just had never impressed her as a man who really got very interested in small children. Of course, Earl had never really had the chance before.

Bill spent most of every day over on Elm Street. Sometimes when he dropped round in the evenings he would roll up his eyes and shake his head over the snail-paced exactitude of the carpenter, and Earl would laugh because he'd warned Bill that old Elmer Shipman was slow.

But progress was definitely being made. Bill took them both over one evening, and afterward, because Helen Fairchild was with his son, he also took them to dinner at the hotel. It was a Friday night so the diningroom was crowded, but the fact that it was Friday was only incidental. Bill hadn't planned it that way. It didn't matter much anyway; everyone around Brunswick had pretty well accepted the fact that Bill Tappan was now one of them and that more often than not when they saw Bill they saw Peggy Wheaton with him.

He'd made some friends, and as a matter of

fact he'd already sold a little legal advice. He did not divulge the nature of it, but over dinner he boasted of having two real, live clients, and Earl laughed.

The only incident that marred their dinner that Friday night was when Peggy gazed casually around the room and saw Harriett's father eating alone. A lot of things rushed back; because Peggy had been so completely preoccupied during Mike's illness, she had completely forgotten about Harriett. But she did not speak to Harriett's father that evening. They exchanged a smile and a nod, but the next morning after Earl had gone and while Bill was busy at the Bellanger place over on Elm Street, Peggy called the drug store.

Harriett's father answered Peggy's inquiry very simply. "She packed up and went over to Boston to get an apartment and look for work. She promised to be home maybe next weekend, Peggy." There was a moment of silence, and then Harriett's father said, "It was all her idea, and I didn't try to stop her. All I said was that if she finds a young man, maybe if she's a little selective, she could find a registered pharmacist. I'd like to retire in a year or two."

Peggy rang off unsure whether to feel pathos or pleasure, whether to be saddened by Harriett's father's loneliness or to be amused by his scheme to get not only his daughter back but to have her bring back someone who was qualified to take over the drug store.

Without being summoned, Helen Fairchild

appeared on the front porch. She said it was
such a beautiful autumn day she thought Peggy
might want to get out for an hour or two.

There was no disputing the quality of the
day, and although Peggy hadn't planned on
going out, it did not take her long to change
into slacks and bulky-knit sweater and leave.

It was a brisk walk from her home to the
north end of Elm Street. She did not go past the
store, not because she didn't want her brother
to see her and interrupt her exercise with
questions but because she preferred the back
streets where there were playing children and
dogs and a different variety of village life than
a person met with over on the commercial
squares.

She smiled at herself. She was getting very
domestic. Or maybe she'd always been domestic
and now she could finally let it surface. She saw
several women she knew and called or waved to
them. They all responded, and at least a couple
of them stood and thoughtfully watched her
stride past. She wondered what married women
with families thought of when they saw an
unmarried girl walk past. She had an idea
about that because, in a sense, she also had a
family.

When she turned in at the brown house,
there were two light trucks out front, one had
the name of the local electrician on the side of
it, the other had the name of the local plumber.
There was another light van in the driveway;
she recognized that one as belonging to Elmer

Shipman. Bill's car was behind the Shipman van.

She went to the open front door, heard men's voices, smelled tobacco smoke and coffee, and overall, the pleasant fragrance of fresh paint. She already knew enough about men to realize that they acted differently without women present than they acted *with* them present, so she stood in the doorway and sang out.

Bill came through from the kitchen in old clothes. His face brightened at the sight of her. He kissed her, then took her by the arm outside. She had expected him to take her on a tour of the house. Instead, he walked her over to the side of his car, where sunshine lay as warm as a benediction, and said, "I had a visitor about an hour ago, the Reverend Muller. I guess it was one of those social calls that may be slightly motivated by proselyting zeal, although he didn't ask my faith or even bring up the subject of religion."

He kept gazing steadily at her. She thought she knew what else he was going to say and held her breath a little hopefully.

"We talked of a lot of things; he was a carpenter once, when he was a young man."

She knew Eric Muller very well. "He was also a sailor once," she said. "Did you like him?"

Bill nodded. "Very much." He paused and looked past, toward the front of the house.

"I—somehow we got on the subject of marriages." His eyes jumped back to her face. "He told me it used to be possible for people to just come by with a ring, but now there are some civil requirements, bloodtests and the like. He said it takes about ten days to get all the paperwork done." He kept looking at her.

She tried to keep her face from showing too much emotion. "It was just a general conversation, then?"

He reached for her hands as he shook his head. "No, I mentioned you and me. He said he had all the forms people have to fill out." His hold on her hands tightened.

"He also said he was at his rectory every night of the week except Friday if we wanted to stop by and talk."

She felt the blurriness coming into her eyes and had to blink it away because they were standing out there in plain sight. "What night?" she asked in a soft voice.

"Tonight?"

She smiled. "Tomorrow night. Tonight, let's just sit by the fire and talk about it between ourselves."

He pecked her on the cheek. "Perfect. Now get in and I'll drive you home."

She shook her head. She knew how that would end if they went back to her house in the emotional state she was now in. "I'll walk back. I like to walk this time of year." She considered kissing him and was deterred by that ugly word they'd used up at the lake: Discipline.

As she freed her hands, she said, "I'll expect you for dinner too, and we'll send Earl off to bed right afterward." She stepped back. He looked at her with a slightly troubled expression, but she only smiled. "Discipline, remember? No kissing in front of the whole town."

She started back the way she had come. She knew he was still standing back there leaning upon the car, watching her. She felt his gaze as a warmly protective shield.

Now the air seemed much clearer, the pale sky was a warmer, more intimate shade of blue, and each breath she took seemed to infuse fresh life and purpose into her. She had often encountered the term "rebirth" but until this afternoon she had not fully appreciated what it meant.

Things she had been seeing all her life around Brunswick, the houses, the fences, the trees, even the few familiar faces she passed and smiled into, were new!

She was tempted to go by the store and tell her secret to Earl, but she didn't. If Harriett had still been around, she would have gone by and told her. But Harriett was gone. That was the one sobering thought on the walk home.

Faith, she told herself, if a person had faith in the basic goodness of life, maybe everything wouldn't turn into a rose garden, but if one kept that thought, it couldn't *hurt*. Harriett would find someone over in Boston. Maybe he would be a pharmacist and maybe he would just be a man whose nerve-ends tingled when he saw Harriett the same way Peggy's did when she saw Bill Tappen, but in any case, it would happen because Peggy would keep the faith for Harriett.

When she reached the house, Helen Fairchild had already seen her striding along out front and was shrugging into her coat at the front door. Helen said, "That boy of yours, Peggy, can think of more reasons why a person should let him out of bed . . ." They laughed and Helen left, and Peggy stood for a moment in the entry-way remembering only part of what Helen had said.

"That boy of yours . . ."

She went to Mike's room. He wriggled all over at sight of her. They hadn't really been friends all that long, but perhaps to a child the length of an acquaintanceship has less to do with it than what has transpired during that friendship, and maybe that was as it should be, too.

Peggy had taken him to her heart with seas of love when he'd arrived in a strange country. She had defended his right to the colors he'd liked when they'd bought his winter clothes; she had given him his room and had been there during his illness whenever he needed someone. Maybe those were the things that made a friendship of only a few weeks seem like a lifetime of friendship.

He started to give her one of his best excuses for getting out of bed as she came over and sat down beside him. She put a cold finger gently over his lips. Then, when he was silent, she leaned, kissed his cheek, felt his forehead and throat for any lingering vestiges of fever, found none, and said, "All right. Tonight when your father comes over, you can go sit with him in front of the fireplace for a little while before you go to bed. And I'll talk to Doctor Benton. If he's willing, you can play a little tomorrow, inside the house. Okay?"

She felt his small hand working across the blankets to her fingers. They clung, and she did not even try to hide from him, this time, the way she felt. She said, "I love you, Mike."

His grip tightened on her fingers, and he looked up at her without speaking, but the expression in his eyes was enough. For a little longer she stayed there; then she had to start dinner. The thought that worked a sobering balance came only gradually: someday, of course, they would have to tell him about his real mother. It wouldn't be easy for her, or for Bill, and it certainly wouldn't be easy for Mike. But she had a number of years between now and then to create a cushion of love between them so that when that day eventually arrived, perhaps he could accept the fact without any deep or serious hurt.

She prayed it could end that way for him.

Promptly at five o'clock Earl arrived. He made them both a drink at the kitchen sideboard, asked casually where Bill was, and then went to visit with Mike. But she halted him at the kitchen doorway.

"I need a favor from you tonight," she said.

Earl swished his highball and gazed back at her. "Don't tell me, let me guess. I'm to eat, then develop an uncontrollable case of the yawns accompanied with drowsiness, and go off to bed early."

She laughed. "You keep surprising me, Earl. How did you know?"

He finished the highball and went back as far as the table to leave the glass before returning to the doorway, where he said, "It's not so hard. Each time you get this way, your eyes sparkle and your face is red."

"It is not!" she exclaimed.

He did not stay and argue; he just gave her a wicked wink and strode on through toward Mike's bedroom.

She went to the mirror in the entry-hall to look. He was right!

She went back to the kitchen and hardly thought any more about herself at all; she thought about *them* . . . the two of them, un' Eric Muller married them. Then there would *three* of them, and maybe after a while, when they were settled over on north Elm Street, four or five of them.